Emerald City

Emerald City

Agnes Vivarelli

Library of Congress Control Number:		2015908326
ISBN:	Hardcover	978-1-5035-0588-9
	Softcover	978-1-5035-0587-2
	eBook	978-1-5035-0586-5

To order additional copies of this book, contact:
Xlibris
1-800-455-039
www.Xlibris.com.au
Orders@Xlibris.com.au
528013

CONTENTS

I dedicate this book to my dad who expired on 16 June 2009.
He didn't talk much. He was an extreme introvert.
My brother and I always said he should have been a lighthouse keeper.
He didn't like talking. I think when he went into the light, back to source,
he would have got a refund on his words; he hardly used any up.

My dad built boats, renovated houses, played guitar,
and sculpted from sandstone.
It is from him I inherit my love of creativity. Thanks, Papabeak!

P. S. Did you stop smoking yet?
I know you can hear me.

BACKWARD

I love a personal story that inspires me and touches my heart. Dr DeMartini once said, 'You don't need to get motivated if you are inspired.'

Motivation says, 'Get up! Go do that.' Inspiration is a push from behind, a rush of energy that is effortless; you are compelled to do it.

There are many books written on motivation. This book is for my inspired flock – you know who you are.

PREFACE

The yellow brick road was the path the characters in *The Wizard of Oz* took to get to Emerald City. They went there to get something they believed they didn't possess. The tin man wanted a heart, the lion wanted courage, the scarecrow wanted a brain, and Dorothy wanted to get back home to Kansas. They believed *The Wizard of Oz* could grant them their wishes. When they got there, they discovered he was just a man behind a curtain, not a wizard at all. Then the fairy godmother showed up with her wand and reminded them, 'You had it in you all along.' She showed them that along their travels, they had showed the qualities they desired to get to the wizard.

The individuals in the thirty-one stories of this book have travelled their own yellow brick road, from non-belief to belief, and they share their stories in detail of how they did it.

This book is for you to remember that you too have always had it in you just like the fairy godmother had said.

Agnes Vivarelli
Apersonofinterest2014@gmail.com
Apersonofinterest.com.au
Agnesvivarelli.com

Double Mani

Desire: New Car/Piano Sale
Time Frame: Nine Months

Over the winter of 2006, the Law of Attraction changed my life for the positive in a mighty way. For more than ten years, I had been co-coordinator of a women's program for victims of domestic violence. I was constantly on the search for new creditable material that would help these women increase their power, self-esteem, and assertiveness while they are going through the anger, grief, all the physical and emotional turmoil of recognising the abusive relationship they are in and either trying to change their perspective so the relationship would work or getting out and rebuilding a healthier lifestyle. At the same time, I was working as a counsellor in a Women's Shelter and teaching RCMP recruits on Domestic Violence. I knew I could make use of what I learnt in all three jobs.

The winter of 2006 found me watching all the professional National Hockey League games that I had time for. One of the commercials during the games was by Kia Automobiles. It constantly showed a Kia Rondo, and I fell in love with it!

At the same time (coincidence?), I was told about another learning tool that another counsellor had read about: the Law of Attraction. I researched and decided at that time that this was something our support group could get into. I ordered the series and for several weeks practiced this on my own. I was then convinced that it could be very beneficial for the group. I introduced it, as much for my benefit as theirs, and we went through one chapter each week.

By now, it was March 2007. I announced to the group about my decision to buy a new 2007 Kia Rondo, burgundy red with grey interior, by the end of the year. I was driving a wonderful car at the time, so why did I think I needed a new one? Hmmm. I did not know at the time that this car would be totalled just two months after I received the new car.

Each week, our support group continued to practice the Law of Attraction. We were all amazed by the positive results. Many of the women were benefitted in so many ways by the action of claiming and then believing they would be receiving. There were winners of door prizes. Many got new jobs. Many wrote their entrance

1

examinations without any fear. Diseases totally disappeared from the point of diagnosis to hospital tests. It was amazing fourteen weeks!

Attendance was never better with everyone jumping with excitement to see what miraculous things happened over the past week. A few of these women were still in the women's shelter, so it didn't take long for word to be out to my other co-workers about the amazing desire I was expecting to manifest.

The support group ended in June 2007, and I didn't think about the car, most of the time. When I did think of it, I would wonder when (and how as I had no money to buy one) I would receive the car. Because I had just said 'by the end of the year', I didn't doubt that it wouldn't happen. I just wondered when and then forgot about it again.

September 2007 saw the beginning of another support group. I was both shocked and totally impressed when my co-facilitator told the group about my new free car manifestation! She remembered my desire better than me! She got the group excited as I sat back smiling at her enthusiasm and the feeling of expectancy that filled the room! How had I managed to forget while my co-worker remembered? I knew the reason was that I didn't need to remember because I had turned it over to the universe. I had let go so I could watch the universe in action. I couldn't believe how calm and assured I was that this really was going to happen – now within four months!

November 2007 found me busy renovating my house on top of the two jobs I maintained. I had no time to get excited about the new car I was expecting. I barely had time to breathe. The support group continued to study the *Law of Attraction* with astounding results. While renovating the house, I received miraculous wisdom for fixing electrical items and drywall, replacing cupboard doors, and so on. Amazingly, I dreamt the solutions! And when I tried the dreams, it worked! How amazing is life when one enters into the realm of manifestation of one's needs and lets it go to watch the results! Blows me away!

On 20 November 2007, I received a phone call from my sister who lived in another province 300 miles away. We were updating each other about the happenings of our grown children. She was complaining that one of her sons was again selling his new car. It had been only seven months since he had bought his car, but now, he had been expecting their fifth child and the car was too small for them. I asked what kind of car it was. She replied, '*2007 Kia Rondo*!' It had been bought brand new, had all the extras, and had gone very few miles. I asked the colour of the car. She said, '*Burgundy red*!' I asked the colour of the interior. She said, '*Grey*!' At this point, my sister asked if I was interested in it. I replied that I might be but had no money, didn't really need a new car, and was far too busy to think of it right now. My heart was racing with the excitement of thinking how close the car was and not knowing how I would end up with it. I was sure this was the car I was supposed to have. I had more difficulty letting go of it then than I had at any point since I had initially made the statement. My stomach was jumping from excitement. I couldn't get the smile off my face. I wanted to jump, shout, and yell a bunch of thank you's to whoever in the universe was listening.

But the phone call wasn't over, and I didn't realise the best was yet to come. It had been said so many times, 'It's better to give than to receive'. I didn't know how fantastic it was going to be until the next part of our conversation. I asked my sister about her youngest son. They had just received the gift of their fifth child and were looking to sell their house so they could afford for him to go back to university to earn the degree that he had started. He had told his mom 'just yesterday' (the previous day of my phone call) that the first thing he wanted to do when he sold the house was to buy his wife a piano. He had promised her one the first year they were married. Five children in six years didn't leave enough money to keep that promise. They now had two daughters ready for lessons, and his wife was really missing having music in the house.

Let me deviate back to September 2007. I was growing tired of 'the same old look' in the house. I decided to sell most of the living room furniture to give more space. This sale included the piano that my folks bought fifty years before for my siblings and me to take lessons. It had been in my home for thirty-two years. It was still in great shape, well-tuned, and a bonus for any home that would make more use of it than I did. I had asked my children and no one wanted it. I advertised this piano for sale several times. I brought the price down each time I advertised. I had, then, given up on the sale as I didn't seem able to give it away! Why didn't the fact that the universe was again in action click me? I only realised just now – yes, seven years later – that the Law of Attraction also wanted to send my piano to my family.

Back to the phone call. When my sister said her son was going to buy a piano, I timidly (almost whispered fearing rejection) asked if she thought he would be interested in our piano. She said, 'You mean ours?'

'Yes.'

'You mean the one from the farm that we took lessons on?'

'Yes.'

'You want to get rid of it?'

'Yes.'

'I think he would be very interested in it! He would love it!'

At this point, she must have been three feet off the floor. Her voice was increasing in both volume and speed. She was getting more excited by the second! She finally asked me why I wanted to sell it. I let her know that I'd had this longing for a while to pass the piano on to someone in the family but no one seemed interested. She let me know in no uncertain terms that her family would be most interested, her son would treasure it like it was worth a million dollars, it would have a prime corner of their house, and I would be thought of, and thanked, every time her daughter-in-law or grandchildren sat down to play it. She finally took a breath and asked if I wanted her son to phone me.

'Yes!'

Within six minutes, I received a phone call from my nephew asking – with disbelief – if it was true that I was selling the family piano. 'Yes.' He asked if he could buy it. 'Yes.' He asked the price. 'Free if you bring the family for a visit.' 'Really?'

'Yes.'

Free to him for the taking. This would be a seven-hour drive, but he was so excited! His wife wanted to leave immediately. I could hear her screaming with excitement in the background. We both agreed that they would do some planning and get back to me.

My nephew was so happy about the piano that I got off the phone and cried. My piano was going to a good home, a home I knew, a home where it would be used and appreciated. Exactly what I had not realised that I called in several months ago!

Ten minutes after the above phone call, I received a phone call from the other nephew. He said his mom had told him that I may be interested in buying his car and he wanted to know if this was true. I said I didn't know (while in my mind, I was telling the universe it had better get busy if this was the car I was supposed to receive). I asked him questions about it. We talked about it a while, and then I asked him to give me two weeks to think about it.

Two weeks later, during a meditation, my mind suddenly stood on end and told me that time was up. I had to phone my nephew. What! I had no money! What would I say? How do I know the universe is reacting to this particular car? Oh heavens, my mind was reeling! I took a firm grip on myself and went back to the meditation. I let the universe know that I was going to say 'Yes', without knowing any details. I also let the universe know that no matter how much I wanted to take over, I wasn't going to. This was now back in the hands of the universe with me *really paying attention*!

I phoned my nephew and told him I would take the car if he would deliver it (over 300 miles). He had no problem with that as my sister had already decided that she was following him out, so she could get in a visit. They had spoken to her other son, and they had all decided to come out together. That way there would be two men to lift the piano out of the house and into the U-Haul. They had been doing all the planning while I was still freaking out about whether I should test the universe and say yes or throw it all out the window by saying no. My gut was saying yes. My mind was telling me that I was crazy.

On 15 December 2007, I was handed a cheque for very close to the price of the car. I just couldn't believe it! I sat for a very long time with my mouth open. I felt my body going from disbelief to shaking with the reality of what was happening right before my eyes. I knew there were close to fifty people waiting to see if this was really going to work. What a testimony! This was no small deal, and I literally floated for the next three months!

On 17 December 2007, I received the car that I had manifested in March 2007. At the same time, my nephew was the recipient of the piano. He had determined that his wife have it after six years of waiting. The universe heard my desire, heard my nephew's desire, wouldn't let me deviate from my original desire, and gave back to me double than what I asked for. Absolutely amazing!

No one believes in the power of the mind more than I have since my introduction to the Law of Attraction.

There is no good among man that pours blessings on the soul more than to give so that others might enjoy a better life!

(Irene Klassen)

ARE WE REALLY DRIVING IN THAT, MUM?

Desire: New Car
Time Frame: One Year

Leaving a long-term relationship is never easy, especially, if you are the one who made the decision. Let me tell you that there is light at the end of the tunnel, and as challenging as things are, it's amazing what you can learn about yourself. They say you never really know how strong you are until you have no choice but to be strong. My life is very different now; however, I just want to share my journey with you. This is one of my experiences that taught me about thoughts and feelings. What you dwell on is exactly what you attract.

My decision was not made lightly; however, it was what I needed to do. I had to remain positive for my two sons aged thirteen and five at the time. I have always taught my boys that out of not so good situations many positive things can happen even though at the time it is very difficult to see. I remember sitting down with my then thirteen-year-old trying to hold myself together and at the same time apologising for my decision. It was at this moment when I realised that everything I had taught this precious young man had actually sunken in. He put his arms around me and said, 'It's OK, Mum. I know you have been unhappy, and if you aren't happy, how can you be the best Mum you need to be for me and my little brother? If this is what you have to do, that is OK because I know we will all be OK if you are OK.' We absolutely were OK, and life was very different now.

I had to go and buy myself a car. So off we went with very limited funds. It did take a few weeks, and there were days of tears because the car I was used to had leather seats and a sunroof. I had moments of shear frustration, and I was being way too picky. I decided to sit down and have an executive meeting with myself. After all, I am the CEO of my life and I needed to start making executive decisions no matter how uncomfortable they were. Really, all I needed was a car that could get me and my boys from A to B, and with the budget I had, there wasn't much available. So we settled on a little two-door Hyundai Excel (1994) model. It had peeling paint on the roof, no airbags or power steering, and no automatic windows or even CD player, all for a grand total of $1,400. What a bargain!

The look on my five-year-old's face was priceless. Then he said, 'Is this really our new car? You can't drive us around in that.' The thing about five-year-old is that they speak exactly what they are thinking. I went on to explain that it didn't cost a lot to run plus it's a bit sporty because it's a two-door car. Then those magic words came out of my mouth, 'Sweetheart, this is only temporary. I promise you that in a year from now, we won't be driving this car.' Right there, at that moment, I spoke those words without even realising that it was my message to the universe. Little did I realise in that split second how powerful those words would actually be. It was a great little car even though it bothered my little one more than it bothered me or my older son. For the first time in many years, I was back in a five-speed manual car, so it was fun explaining to my boys how the gear change works and how to slow down using the brakes (good lessons from my dad who was a truck driver). We had a few expenses; however, we always managed to get by.

Now when I think back about that car, I also think of all those times when I told my boys, 'This is not forever. I know it's not your ideal car, but it will do for now.' I was always looking in the paper for something better; however, it was a bit silly thinking and looking at newer cars when I could not afford to pay for one. I continued to do this every other day, even at the time I knew deep down a new car was a little out of reach. I never ever said it. I actually did more imagining that we would all be driving a new one sooner rather than later.

This is where things get interesting. My car was due for registration in October 2009 as I had purchased the car in October 2008, and it had just been registered prior to me buying it. It was the week the registration was due, and I remember picking up my little guy from school and going home doing my usual, that is park the car in the driveway. On that day, I think I had been home about half an hour, and there was a knock on my door. I opened the door, and there was my neighbour. All I heard was, 'Your car has rolled into our house'. OMG! Luckily, her children were not playing in the front yard, and there were no cars on the road when my little Hyundai rolled down my driveway. To this day, I still have no idea how! However, I think the poor little car just gave up because of the constant talk about getting a new one.

My car was a right off, and it was pointed out to me by a friend that I had been talking about a new car since I got that one. The universe really does deliver, *ask, believe,* and *receive.* The upside to all of this was that my neighbours started renovating soon after, and they thanked me because that little accident got them started. I got more money back for the car than I had paid, which was a bonus. I decided to go to my bank and see if this single mum could get a personal loan.

Earlier in the year, I had applied for a $500 credit card for emergencies, and it was granted. I made a point that if I ever used it; I would never add another thing until the first thing was paid off in full. This good habit showed my bank that I could manage my money, and I was granted a $10,000 loan for a newer car. We bought a 2005 model Holden ASTRA with airbags, power steering, and electric windows. My next car will be the one with the leather seats and sunroof. My eldest son is eighteen and has his own car now, and my little guy is ten and he loves my car.

So what I really want to get across from this story is the power of belief. I promised my boys that within a time frame, we would have a newer car. However, with no clear idea how! I held onto that belief. I remained grateful for the car I had even though it wasn't perfect. I had a clear vision of the new car and me behind the wheel. Looking at new cars in the paper became a ritual even though a new car was unaffordable at the time. When I thought about the possibility of a new car, it gave me the most amazing feeling, you know like the 'warm fuzzies.' This is so important to attach a feeling to your desires. They become so much more powerful. Yes, there were those times where a little doubt crept in; however, I was always aware of these feelings, so if that ever happened, I would go look at another picture and write in my gratitude journal how grateful I was to have a new car. Those 'warm fuzzies' came flooding back. Manifesting your desires requires consistency, unshakeable belief, and total trust and surrender to the entire process. Your desires are only delivered when you are totally ready to receive them. I have taught both my boys these processes, and when you see them using these principles to manifest their own desires, that is really exciting. My ten-year-old calls it, 'The Force' (a big *Star Wars* fan), and he gets it. Since this story, I have manifested my dream partner and together we manifested our home (no more renting to pay for someone else's dream). This is so much more than positive thinking even though that has a lot to do with it. These principles are life changing if you are willing to just *ask, believe, and receive.* Repeat again and again. You just have to trust the process, have fun, and enjoy every minute of attracting your desires.

The Law of Attraction is just so powerful. *What you dwell on is what you attract!*

Carol Johnston: Author, Empowerment/Self Esteem, Law of Attraction Life Coach.

Creator of Buds To Blossoms: Empowerment for Girls and Mothers and Daughters United.

www.caroljohnston.com.au
email: carol@caroljohnston.com.au

TOWNHOUSE IN ASHGROVE

Desire: Buying a Townhouse
Time Frame: Six Years

Well, I have many stories I could tell that are tied into the idea of putting the intention out there and watching the universe bring it into actualisation. I've picked up work in the Arts Industry as a student to the amazement of my peers. I've also changed career paths utilising the power of intention and in full awareness of the workings of the Law of Attraction. And, last year, I manifested a trip to the Melbourne Cup including airfares from the Sunshine Coast and accommodation in Melbourne CBD. But the story I'd like to share now is one about our townhouse purchase.

In early 1998, my husband and I decided to commit and purchase our first property. This in itself was an example of the Law of Attraction. I was working for a financial planner, and when I mentioned to him we wanted to buy a place, he told me to set up a savings account and within two or three years, we'd be set. We'd been spending weekends doing open houses and had a fair idea that we wanted a unit or a townhouse close to Brisbane CBD but only in the Western suburbs. So, yes, we were clear on what we wanted and two years seemed like a very long time to wait. We didn't have much savings, but my motto is 'where there's a will there's a way,' and we managed to borrow from willing parents (we later paid them back) and got together enough to get a deposit and secure bank finance.

One Saturday, during our usual weekend real estate inspections, we happened to wander through a new townhouse complex in Ashgrove, newly built and being sold by the developer, and we fell in love with a four-bedroom townhouse in the complex that still had yet to have carpets laid. It was significantly out of our price range. Well, that's what we told ourselves. We were really just looking to get an idea of what you could get in that price range to compare it to the price range we had committed to with our budget. We fantasised about owning it but really didn't believe it was possible in that moment, so we just crossed it off the list. However, to make ourselves feel better, we agreed that it was the type of place we wanted to own in our next purchase.

On Anzac Day, 25 April 1998, we 'settled' on a two-bedroom unit in Milton. Don't get me wrong. I really loved that unit and was very grateful for it, and we enjoyed making it ours. But in the back of our minds, we know this was temporary. I lost count of the number of times I said, 'Our next property will be a townhouse in Ashgrove!' I even wrote it down on a goal list with no date in mind. But in our minds, it wasn't just any townhouse in Ashgrove.

So life kept moving. My husband was offered a job in Switzerland, and we relocated in mid-2000. We tried to sell our unit in Milton for a number of months, but finally, annoyed by the offers we were getting – and I'm sure, by divine intervention – we decided to take it off the market and rent it. A psychic at the time told me the universe was looking after me and that we would return to Australia sooner than we expected and the property would be worth more. Not that I really believed him or trusted in the process in that moment.

We returned to Brisbane in March 2003. I was pregnant with our first child. We moved back into our unit in Milton. We figured, while it was OK for the time being, it was ultimately too small to accommodate our new 'working from home' status and growing family, so, of course, we started fantasising again about a particular townhouse in Ashgrove. We had a look around to see what was on the market and nothing seemed suitable, and it was then I realised that property prices had escalated and we were grateful that we had kept our unit.

When we decided to sell our Milton unit at the end of 2003, we received almost double the amount of the best offer we had received in 2000! We would not have saved that in three years. Well, not with the travel we'd been doing. Things also worked well for us, in that, our unit was purchased by an investor, and she was happy to rent it back to us until we found our next property. We were struggling to find something suitable despite a lot of looking.

Deciding one day to widen the search price parameters, we discovered the townhouse we saw in 1998 was back on the market. It was outside of what we hoped to pay, but we couldn't resist going and having a look. Well, I don't think it was possible mentally and energetically for us to create space for another property despite the fact that we looked at a three-bedroom townhouse that was in our price range, in Ashgrove, in close proximity that same day.

Emotionally, we knew what we wanted. How frustrating (note this was my dominant vibration here) to be in the same situation again looking at this townhouse, wanting it to be ours but still not believing it was possible for us to afford it! Thankfully, our finance broker convinced us that we could afford it and that he could get the finance for us. What followed was a two-week period of interesting exchange that I can only describe as a reflection of our lack of trust in the process of life and the universe. Our doubt certainly created a vibrational flow that was in resistance, and our next challenge was when we decided to make an offer to purchase the townhouse, we were told there was a contract already on the townhouse but it was subject to sale of another house. We just had to wait for the contract to lapse. It felt like 'time out to think about what we were doing wrong!' That contract did lapse, and we signed a contract, but we still had the small issue of finance approval because we didn't have tax returns due to our stint in Switzerland, so we had to be approved through a different financing process. It was literally eleventh hour on our 'subject to finance' clause, and we were still faxing documents to our broker as he tried to work with the bank to get us over the line. Through this time, we held the vision of living in that townhouse. In our mind, there was no other option.

Our contract settled, and we picked up the keys on 12 February 2004. We were so grateful that at last it was ours, and it only took us six years to allow it into our life, but the Law of Attraction and the universe is patient. It truly is the doubt that sets up the resistance that slows down the manifestation. These days, rather than saying, 'We can't afford that!' my preference is 'What would it take to have it?'

Even my husband is starting to believe that it's possible to work with the Law of Attraction, especially when looking for a car park in a busy shopping centre, but that's another story.

Jillian Jones – www.JillianJones.com

INVESTMENT PROPERTY SALE POP'S LEGACY

Desire: Sale of House
Time Frame: Six Weeks

From the moment I was born, I had always had a very special bond with my grandfather, and so did my sister when she came along. As children growing up, Nan and Pop were always in our lives, and for that, I have been forever grateful. My grandmother passed away when I was twelve years old; however, I was lucky enough to have my grandfather for a lot longer. He was there with me and witnessed many of my significant life events. He also had a beautiful relationship with my two boys (his great-grandsons). My youngest son Nicholas used to call him 'Poppy white hair', and when we would visit him, there were many times where he would be sitting out on my mother's veranda deep in conversation with my eldest son Luke.

After my grandmother passed away, Pop lived on his own for quite a few years. He managed remarkably well; however, he did spend a lot of time at my parent's house. Pop was my dad's dad. In around 1993 (I can't remember the exact year), Pop had to have a cataract operation, so while he was recovering, he stayed with my parents. After his second operation, he never went back home. He rented out his house and moved in with Mum and Dad. My dad was an interstate truck driver, so Pop being there for Mum when Dad was away worked out really well. (My sister and I had left home at this stage). It was so lovely that my parents and grandfather had such a wonderful relationship.

In May 2000, my dad passed away unexpectedly at the age of fifty-four. Having my grandfather living with Mum actually helped their grieving process; however, regardless of the age, no parent ever wants to outlive their children. My sister and I were so glad that they had each other. I was living in the Central Coast, and my sister was in Sydney. As the years went on, Pop happily stayed with Mum; however, his health started to deteriorate, and in April 2008, two days before my thirty-eighth birthday, we lost Pop too. He had been in a hospital with a chest infection. I was very blessed to get to talk to him on the phone that afternoon. (We regularly spoke on the phone every Sunday, which I had always done with my mum since I left home in 1986.) I clearly remember having this lovely chat with him and at the same time thinking how wonderful he sounded. Our conversation finished as it did every Sunday with 'I love you, Pop,' and he would say, 'Love you too.' I got the call at nine o'clock that night. He was ninety-seven years old. To this day, I miss both Pop and Dad; however, I am so grateful to have them for the time that we did. In my dad's case, fifty-four is way too young to die and too soon to leave the family. I have found it so much harder dealing with my father's passing; however, with Pop, I am totally ok with it as he had a very happy and long life. My two boys and my sister's three girls were all significant in his life, and we are grateful for that.

Our darling grandfather had left my sister and me a house in his will. He had always said to us that he wanted us both to be secure and own our own homes, and this was his way of leaving a legacy so that we could. The house had actually been in our family for more than sixty years. It was old; however, it had a really good tenant. We had no mortgage, so we decided to keep it and see what happened.

One day, I was having a discussion with my sister about the house, just in regard to what we might do with it. We decided that we would have a five-year plan, hold onto it for at least five years, and see how we feel then. We treated the house as a compulsory savings fund, and the only time we took money from our rent account was at Christmas time. It paid for presents and for all our Christmas food. My sister, mum, and our families always spend Christmas together, so at every Christmas lunch, we all would say, 'Thank you, Poppy.' Luckily, over the course of time, there wasn't any need to do too much work for the house except the normal maintenance stuff.

My sister and I regularly talked about the five-year plan as we both felt it was a good time frame to hold onto the house. Moreover, five is my favourite number. My sister and her husband have been renting for a long time, so eventually; this house would enable them to get a deposit for their first family home just like Pop wanted. In 2012, my partner and I were fortunate enough to be able to buy a home together, and I remember saying to my sister that when we would sell our little house, it would really help with my mortgage. In November 2012, my partner and I took a little trip to visit my mum and organised to do an inspection on our little house. As 2013 would be five years since we had owned it, I thought it would be a good time to have a look, see what needed to be done, and get an appraisal just to see what we might be able to sell for. I will not forget that day. The tenant was a truck driver, and his mother had rented it before him. We knew he wasn't there much, but I was not prepared for the shock and disappointment I got when I walked through the back door. The house was a mess. I had never seen it look like that before. The walls were filthy. There was a hole in the roof, there was wood rot in the bathroom, and some of the windows had been nailed shut. To make matters even more interesting, I had made an appointment for an agent to come and look at the property. (How embarrassing!) I was just devastated. The agent wasn't fazed by it. He informed me he had seen houses that were worse than our little house.

Donna (my sister) and I had been trying to decide if we should put a new roof on prior to selling. This is where the agent comes in because we thought we would consider it if it was going to add significant value. However, the agent advised that the price range would barely change with or without a new roof and considering the damage we may have to get those things fixed first before even putting the house on the market. I was quite emotional about everything because of the sentimental value and attachment I had to this house. The following day, I met with the tenant to discuss what was to happen going forward and my disappointment in the state of the house. During our discussion, he informed me that he had planned to move out in January. This could actually work in our favour. So when I got back home, I spoke to my sister and showed her the photos I had taken (which upset her as much as it upset me). We decided to start getting quotes and getting the things done that needed urgent attention. We also decided to write to our tenant and give him notice to be out by the second week in January 2013 so that we could all go up and clean the house and start getting it ready to go on the market. It was in this short period of time things got really interesting.

I had gotten myself so worked up and upset about the house that I had to sit down and take stock of what I was feeling. Because of the emotional attachment, I had to detach myself from the house.

The Law of Detachment had to come into play here: I had to put faith and trust in the final outcome no matter how we got there. Although, this was a successful, easy sale at the right price, I don't want to dwell on it too much. Detachment means trusting the outcome will happen one way or another. If you are too attached and by this I mean we need the sale, we need the money, you will stay in a state of need, thus pushing the outcome further away.

So basically we just got on with living our lives and sent the letter to the tenant, and he agreed to be out on the weekend we had chosen. All was good, so we just started preparing for Christmas. On 21 December, I got a phone call from the tenant's mother enquiring about our selling price because she knew someone who may be interested. I told her to give them my details and I would talk them.

That was a significant day as it was that fateful day when the world was supposed to end; however, the real meaning of that was the new beginning. Now I had a new focus. It looked like the universe was really listening. The following day, I had a phone call from a man who lived behind the house, and he informed me that his brother in Sydney may be interested in purchasing the house. I had already spoken to my sister, and we agreed that we would give him a ballpark price slightly higher than what the real estate agent had appraised if the issue of price came up which it did. With Christmas so close, we knew we wouldn't be able to do too much; however, I had a lovely chat with the man who was interested and organised to show him the property the same weekend the tenant was moving out.

So now I really had to focus on the Law of Allowing: this was to let it be, let it all flow, and just let the universe deliver. Have faith that this sale was now inevitable.

Christmas came and went, and in no time at all, it was time to head up north and show the man the house. My sister and I decided to take all the children and visit Mum for a few days. Our partners were going to follow a little later. No sooner had I pulled into my Mum's driveway, my phone rang and it was Charlie (potential buyer) just letting us know he had arrived and couldn't wait to see the house. We had arranged for him to see it the following day. During the course of the evening, Donna and I were discussing every scenario that we thought may happen. We had discussed our top price that we wanted and our bottom price. So we were organised, scared, and excited considering we were doing this all on our own with no agent which we knew would save us a lot of money. The following day, we had to do a few things for Mum, and while we were out, I got a call from another person wanting to look at the house to potentially buy; however, I informed him that Charlie had driven from Sydney and he was looking first. Funny thing was that I had a weird feeling about the other fellow, so I decided that he wasn't going to be our buyer. The day passed quickly, and it was time to meet Charlie at the house. We were so nervous, trying to remain cool, calm, and collected.

He was the loveliest man. He walked around. We showed him all the worst bits first, and to our surprise, it didn't faze him what so ever. He told us that his son was a builder and the house had massive potential and then he spoke the magic word. He said, "Well, darling girls, how does $$$$$ sound to you both?' I looked at Donna trying to keep calm. We both nodded to each other and said, 'Yes, that is great.' He had offered the exact price we wanted at the top of our range. No negotiation whatsoever. We exchanged details to get the ball rolling after the New Year. The rest is history. We finalised everything in February 2013, which was exactly to the end of our five-year plan.

I have to say, I absolutely believe that this whole process was divinely guided from the moment we decided we could keep the house for five years the wheels were already in motion, right down to the timing of the tenant moving out or indicating he wanted too. In the end, we didn't spend a cent on repairs except for a water pipe and tap on the hot water system.

We truly believe that our father and grandfather had a hand in choosing the buyer. The buyer was a retired fellow who was planning on restoring his new home back to its former glory.

So remember the Law of Detachment works hand in hand with the Law of Allowing. My sister has her house deposit, and my mortgage is a little lighter. Thank you, Pop.

Caroljohnston.com.au
Email: carol@caroljohnston.com.au

TRIP TO VEGAS

Desire: Trip to Vegas
Time Frame: One Year

It all started one day in September 2013, when I heard my favourite classic rock station ask, 'Would you like to win a trip to Las Vegas?'

To which I instantly replied to whoever could hear me, 'Well, of course, I would. Are you nuts?'

The announcer then proceeded to explain that several times during the week they would announce the contest and you had to be the tenth caller in order to get your name in the drawing. Then, on a specific day in October, you had to be listening at a specific time, and if your name was drawn, you had ten minutes to call them up and claim your trip.

I thought about it for a few minutes, imagining myself winning, and how much fun it would be for my sweetie and me to go to Vegas. I hadn't been there since I took my daughter for her twenty-first birthday and that was over eight years ago, and he had never been to Vegas at all. It was definitely time.

So right then and there I decided that the contest had been announced for me. I wanted to win the trip to Las Vegas.

I immediately started to prepare.

I checked my calendar to make sure I didn't already have something planned for the date of the trip. (The radio station had a specific date on which you must take the trip.) I didn't have anything scheduled, so I wrote, 'Going to Las Vegas.'

Then I put the date in my phone calendar with an alert to remind me to be up early on the day of the drawing so I could be listening and prepared to call in when they drew my name.

Next, I contacted my nephew to see if he could run my retail shop while I was away. Then I ordered a free copy of the Las Vegas Visitor's Guide online so that I could start planning my activities right away.

I was really excited! Woo hoo! We were going to Las Vegas!

Each time the radio announcer gave the cue, I kept on calling. It actually took me about three weeks before I was finally the tenth caller, and my name was included in the drawing. I felt so confidant I would win. Every time I heard them announce another contestant's name, I just thought about Vegas and how fun it would be.

The Wednesday morning of the drawing, I got up early and tuned it. Sure enough, the DJ announced, 'A**** Miller, you are the winner and have ten minutes to call us and claim your trip.' *What? A. Miller? I'm Kathleen Miller.* Hmmm, I must admit I had a moment of disappointment.

Then suddenly, I got really excited because I realised I was only half a name away from winning. I know it sounds crazy, but I actually jumped up and down in excitement because I was so close. That meant the universe was working on it, and it was on the way! I celebrated the closeness of the match.

After that, I just let it go. When my Las Vegas Visitor's Guide arrived in the mail, I looked through it still thinking I would love to take my sweetie to Vegas. Who knows? All possibilities exist.

A couple of weeks went by, the weather turned colder, and it was close to the date I had marked 'going to Las Vegas' in my calendar. I admit, I felt kind of down and a wee bit cranky when I saw it right there in print, in my calendar, reminding me I was not the winner.

Knowing that what I am feeling is what I am vibrating and attracting, I knew I needed to find some way to shift into 'a better feeling place'. So I decided to go home from work, relax, kick off my shoes, sip some hot coffee (it was already snowing here), and enter some online sweepstakes while listening to Christmas music. I just love Christmas music. It always makes me feel good. So for about the next hour, that's what I did. It felt like inspired action.

I subscribe to a sweepstakes newsletter online, so I entered for all kinds of things: cars, trips, computers, cash, etc. I find it lots of fun to enter because there's always the possibility you may win. I love that feeling, hopeful and full of possibilities. After all, you have to enter to win.

I went on about my routine after that, never giving it anymore thought. Then on Wednesday, 12 December, I received a phone call to verify that I was indeed Kathleen Miller, birth date, etc., because I was the grand prize winner of a trip to Las Vegas!

Am I excited? Absolutely! Am I surprised? Not at all. Why? Because I was really clear about what I wanted. I had imagined how much fun it would be and vibrationally aligned with that. I prepared to receive it and took inspired action. I didn't let not winning the trip from the radio station shift me back into 'reality'. I celebrated the closeness of the match, instead.

The universe delivered back to me what I had visualised, and it was even better. I get to choose when I want to go. I chose to go on the trip the 26 September 2014.

Way to go universe, that's the way I like to roll!

Kathleen Miller
LuckyLifeCoach@aol.com
www.LuckyLady711.com

UNIVERSE KNOWS BEST

Desire: To Get Out of Financial Mess
Time Frame: A Year

I am sure that what I experienced in 2007 was to get me on my path to helping people change their lives.

My family and I moved to Australia from London. Our house had just been built, and we were doing the landscaping and finishing touches and enjoying spending time settling our children and us into our new life.

My husband and I went to the bank to get some money out, and we were asked by the cashier if we would like to see a financial advisor as we had money that could be making us much more money rather than just being in our account.

Over the coming weeks, we saw the financial advisor quite a few times, and based on his professional advice, we ended up putting our money in the stock market, and because of the tax benefits suggested by him, we borrowed money to put in there as well.

I got a part-time job, but it was proving much harder for my husband to find work, but the advisor told us that we would be making enough money each month from the stock market and it would take the pressure off my husband looking for work as we would be receiving an income. During this time, I had no feelings or indication not to do this, and generally, my feelings have been a very good guide for me.

As we all know, the Global Financial Crisis started in 2008, and the money we invested plummeted, and over the next few months, we started to realise we were in big trouble. The advisor kept telling us we were fine and not to worry, and I would lie awake at night for hours feeling the energy building in my chest and filling my body with anger and fear. I knew my husband was awake too, but I didn't want to move or put a voice to the fears going around in my head. I never got up; I just used to lie there, angry, agitated, and scared.

This went on for weeks, and then we started getting letters telling us that if we didn't make payments towards the loan, we could lose our home. This situation was affecting us very badly. I was really worried about my husband's state of

19

mind, and he would also get terrible tension headaches. I would phone home at different times of the day to make sure he was OK. We had gone from being very financially secure to potentially losing everything. I felt it was my fault as I had been the one who had wanted to move here. My husband had left an excellent job in the UK so we could immigrate, and now, I had two jobs and he still couldn't get work and he was just helping someone deliver leaflets to take his mind off what was happening to us.

I was irritable and emotional, and I couldn't think straight. We didn't tell any of our family or friends what was going on. We just kept it between us.

One day, my friend had a psychic come to her house to give readings, so I went to see if he could tell me what would happen to us. He told me he had never seen such a strong indication that someone was starting their spiritual journey, and I remember thinking, 'What a waste of time! That's not what I want to know.' I also thought that he must be crazy as I was quite left brained and other than seeing a psychic and having Reiki a few times, I didn't know very much about that way of life. I also had a belief that spiritual people were very gifted and you could only do these things if you were born with this gift. I now know that we are all born with it, but most of us turn it off ourselves.

So life went on, and I remember praying to my Nan and Grandad in heaven or anyone who was listening to me out in the universe to help us. A few weeks later, my friend gave me a book to read, and something clicked within me and I started reading everything I could about spirituality, energy, and the Law of Attraction. I started to try to change my thoughts and see in my mind this stressful situation as if it had been dealt with. I made promises to the universe that I would change and be thankful every day for peace of mind and the freedom we have. I tried to stay more positive and started to tell my husband about how important our thoughts are and that they do create our reality. I started to notice a difference in how I was thinking and dealing with the situation, and then one day, my prayers were answered. Two angels (I will call them that) who worked at the bank were assigned to help us, and they realised we should never have been allowed to take out the loan in the first place, as we would be unable to repay the loan as my salary would not cover it if needed. We still took a big loss financially, but we were out of the mess and our home was safe.

I continued reading books and going to different events and finding out about so many wonderful things, but I wasn't really doing anything with the information or sharing it with others, even though it had helped us in an amazing way.

I had friends start to say to me I should do healings, but I was too shy and the belief I shared earlier was still strong. That was until Ella, our dog, came into our lives. We were told she probably only had three weeks to live as she had cancer, and my heart melted. I studied healing modalities and practiced on her as she was my perfect patient and her health started to improve. She had a sparkle in her eye and more energy again, and that was in 2011, and she is still with us today. She has been one of my teachers, and I have found that other teachers come into my life to teach me different modalities at the right time. I find that when I am stuck, it's because I am pushing for something that is not the right path for me, and when I let it go, what I need to do falls smoothly back into place.

I work as a Medical Intuitive Practitioner, and I work with people to realign their energy and support them to let go of the story that's causing the pain or discomfort so they can heal. The great thing is most of the time they don't know what's caused the problem and just by having the healing helps to release it.

By going through what had happened to us, I had realised that everything that happens to us in life is a story and how the energy from that story builds in our aura and body and can create chronic pain, disease, or stress within us. When we let go of the story, the pain, disease, etc., are released and our body can become healthy again. I am sure that if I had not taken the opportunity to start on this spiritual path when I did and let go of the fear and anger of losing our money, the energy within me would have caused an illness or disease.

It really is amazing what can happen to us. There is a reason for everything, and if I hadn't gone through this experience, I wouldn't love doing what I am doing and helping other people to be healthy and happy. Thank you, xx!

Ann Harris
www.opulentsouls.com

DREAMING MY HOME

Desire: Buying a Home
Time Frame: Eight Months

As a young child, I knew very early on that I wanted a property in the Bay of Islands, New Zealand, to have as my own. The closest I came to this dream was by looking at real estate books.

I never really got any closer than that, and I now know why: I did not *believe* that I could achieve it; I did not think I was worthy.

I am just like everyone else with dreams and goals, hoping, wishing, and looking at what other people had, wondering how they did it, and deep down inside wanting to be them, but not knowing how to start or what to do, and underneath it all not really believing that I could have what I most desired.

In 2013, my journey truly began. I enrolled in a course that changed my belief system and taught me to *believe* no matter what. So I was going to make sure that I soaked up everything and everybody. Along with the course, there was (and still is) a support network with like-minded and amazing people on the same journey.

To connect with them, all I had to do was join Face book and so I did. This was not easy for me, as I am a rather private person and this was really stretching me.

However, this time it was different – *very* different. I felt that I needed to prove to myself, my family, and the universe that I was serious and committed to the complete process. I wanted to be held accountable. This scared the crap out of me!

What if I did not achieve this goal and desire? What will everyone think of me? That's the problem when we dream and then undream (if that's a word). It is like opening a door and then suddenly closing it and saying to the universe, 'No'.

(The universe does not know what the hell you want. You need to be clear and stay clear. That is what I had just learnt and so it was time to *believe*.)

So I put my intention out there to show how serious I was and to make it so.

In June 2013, Agnes posted an adventurous goal on the ISCA Facebook page, putting it out there for everyone to see and declaring it to be achieved by the end of the year. She challenged other people to do the same. I thought *I can do that!* It did take me a couple of hours to reply and do the same, so here it is for the world to see:

To purchase a property in the Bay of Islands, New Zealand, a place where my husband and I will move to permanently within the next two to three years. I have my mind set on the year 2015. I want this property to be self-sustainable as possible, and most of all, I want to be the caretaker and nurturer of this piece of earth for generations to come. To be achieved by the end of 2013.

No pressure!

I am a big believer in the Law of Attraction: what you put out is what comes back. Your thoughts *are* your future. I am also a huge fan of manifesting and affirmations, and these were the tools I intended to use to make my dream come true.

You have to know we did not have a deposit saved up at the time, but that was not going to stop me. I kept saying, *The money will be there! The money will be there!* I declared to the world what was my heart's desire, so off I went believing in it.

So I started with my grateful journal every night before I went to bed. I would record things for which I was grateful throughout my day and added my dream to my list as if it was already so (five to ten minutes).

I am grateful now that I have purchased our property in Helena Bay, New Zealand.

I had seen this particular property the last time my husband and I were in New Zealand, and I knew then that this was the one. I wanted to be specific to the universe and so named the area. Then down the track, I got the address and added this in as well.

I then used visualisation in my meditations every morning. When I was in a deep state, I would visualise myself sitting on the hill on the property, looking out over the trees and noticing how green the grass was. This was my happy place – my sacred place – in my meditations (five to twenty minutes).

I would daydream throughout the day while sitting at the lights in the car, lying in bed at night, walking in the morning, and even in the shower! I imagined myself and my husband sitting out on our patio on the property having breakfast or lunch, playing with our dogs (we don't even have any of these yet!), doing the gardening, building our home, or watching the sun go down after a day of working on the land with a glass of wine (we do have lots of this!). This was true bliss for me (less than five minutes).

I wrote affirmations on Post-it notes and put these up above my computer and on my mirror above my basin so I could see these everyday while brushing my teeth (one to two minutes).

I spoke about it to anyone that was interested. This built up energy and made me feel happy and helped with the belief feeling. That is where the true magic happens – in the *feeling.*

I created a visualisation board for the next twelve months, and on it was the house I wanted to build and a picture of the exact piece of land I wanted, even a picture of the horse I dream of (one hour and ongoing).

Now I know you may be looking at all of this and thinking, *How did she learn these things? Where did she get the time? If I want to do the same, where do I start?* So I say to you, with lots of love, just take one step at a time. Read books, arm yourself with knowledge, hang out and connect with people who are like-minded, focus and believe in your dream and in your desire, and then *act* on your dream. Some of these tools I used took me less than five to ten minutes per day.

Now I waited over three months before I decided it was time to make the offer on the property, and guess what? The deposit came to us from a much unexpected source! So that's when I knew it was time to move forward. Not once did I think it would be sold to someone else. I had a sense that it was waiting for me, waiting for us. It's funny how sometimes you just *know*. So we made an offer, and after another couple of months of negotiations, it was all signed and accepted in December 2013. (Goal achieved in divine time!) I was over the moon, elated, and probably a little shocked and couldn't quite believe it. When the property settled and the keys were in my hand, my manifestation – which was always true – became real to me.

Marlene Richardt
marlene@links4life.com.au
links4life.com.au

Marriage Made in Heaven

Desire: Marriage/Husband
Time Frame: Two Months

When I was in my mid-thirties, I really started thinking about marriage. I had longed for it when I was younger too; however, circumstances in my life caused me to move into a direction of self-love and value, so marriage was not on my mind for several years.

I knew exactly what type of man I wanted, and at this time, I discovered that writing things down in my journal worked really well for me when I wanted to visualise something. I had recently read a good article by my friend and mentor John Randolph Price, and I wanted to incorporate what I learned from him into what I wrote.

All of the first three steps I said aloud.

First: I set my intention and said aloud, 'It is my intention to be a radiating and attracting centre of the divine energy of a marriage made in Heaven.'

Second: I stated how this marriage should be: 'The Divine Energy of a marriage made in Heaven is a marriage with great communications. This is a marriage with great love, a sense of adventure, a marriage that will last a lifetime. I see this as marriage that is peaceful, joyful, and fun.' I visualised these energies pour into me.

Third: This step was very important for me. 'What I see for myself I see for *all* others.' I would then visualise this Divine Energy of a marriage made in Heaven for my city, for my state, for my country, and for my world. I would see each step of this just as radiating light pouring out. This made me feel very happy to think that we all would be in our perfect relationships; the world would be at peace. I would see people as couples all over the world, especially in countries that were in difficult times.

Fourth: Now I got quiet. I pictured myself as a projector, and I then pictured scenes in my mind. One of them was me in the church getting married. I just saw my husband as a beam of light. I then pictured myself running out of the church and jumping into a limousine with all my friends to go celebrate. Then I pictured many other scenes that I wanted to be doing with my husband.

Fifth: I expressed great gratitude for what was going to take place.

Now during the day, anything that upset me or caused me discomfort, I would radiate out the Divine Energy of a marriage made in Heaven to whatever or whoever it was. This immediately made me feel really good, like I was on a mission for planet Earth.

Two months later, as I was walking with a group of friends into the movie theatre, I was hit by cupid's arrow. That was literally what it felt like, and I was instantly in love with one of my friends that was in the group. I hadn't thought of him this way because he had a girlfriend and she was my friend too. Eight months later, we were married. His girlfriend married someone else in our group too. We remained great friends. Now, what is cool about this story is that when I visualised myself running out of the church and hopping into the limousine with my friends, he was always in the limousine in the group of friends!

We were not married in a church but in front of a beautiful fountain outside of where I worked, by a judge that I knew, surrounded by friends and family.

Marriage is an interesting road, and I would love to tell you that it has always been perfect however it hasn't but that is what a marriage made in Heaven is all about. Because when you marry the right person, you are there for each other through thick and thin, through children, through losing your parents, or through illnesses. There might be stress or some angry words, but you are still there for each other as my husband has been for me and me for him. We will be celebrating our twenty-first anniversary this August, and not only do we live together, but we have also worked together for the past twenty years.

God is so good, life is so wonderful, and my marriage made in Heaven is so richly blessed!

Vanessa Compton
philandvanessa@att.net

THE LAW OF ATTRACTION REALLY WORKS

Desire: Health
Time Frame: Nine Years

In both the negative and positive sense, the Law of Attraction has been proven in my life. In 2005, I was working two part-time jobs. That May, when I received my monthly roster for my second job, I discovered that they had given me one day off for the whole month. One day! Not enough time off to recharge my energy! Admittedly, most days had only one or two hours' work, often in the evenings, but still there's no mental time out for me.

One Friday, I had the evening off after working in the morning and a late start the next day. So I decided it was a good time to get away for a few hours.

On the way out of town, I called in at the offices of my second job. Three administration staff were there, including the general manager. I tried to discuss my roster issue with them, and it seemed they wouldn't listen. I said, 'If you keep treating your staff this way, you'll burn them out.' No response. So I said, 'You could kill people like this.' Still no response. So I repeated myself. The third time I said, 'You'll kill me!' All three of them turned their attention to me, and I thought, 'Uh-oh, what have I done!'

I went out and partied with some friends out of town, and it seemed I had a wonderful time, although I remember very little of it. I woke up five weeks later in Intensive Care at a major metropolitan hospital to be told that I had died five times!

I was a passenger in a car which hit a tree. My injuries were mostly caused by the seatbelt, which incidentally prevented me from flying through the windscreen and dying on impact. I had sustained a broken neck, badly damaged shoulder, and bursting of small intestine.

Not only had I died and revived five times, but also had fifteen major operations, tubes and bags everywhere, and bolts in my head for halo traction,

27

and I was confined to bed for two more months. I couldn't hold up a book or computer to read, and I lost my hearing, so television or music was no consolation.

So I focused on healing my body. As I lay there, I imagined cells dividing. I brought white light and healing energy to my neck and belly, especially. I thanked my lucky stars for having a rich inner life and being a dreamer.

It was an amazing experience, almost a rebirthing, being spoon-fed by my mum. After some weeks, I regained movement in my shoulder.

My little niece, having overheard a conversation, said to me, 'You know you're going to be in a wheelchair?' I responded, 'Is that right?' I told myself I didn't have to believe that. So I didn't. The first steps I took were so painful I cried.

Nine years later, I'm almost as good as I was. I am convinced that what I believe has enormous influence on my life. I am grateful for the experience as it has caused me to find my creative abilities.

Irene Ackland
ireneackland@gmail.com

Australia Home

Desire: Moving to Australia
Time Frame: Two Years

I had dreamt of moving to Australia since first visiting there when I was nineteen. Fast forward to around age twenty-seven, when a friend of mine introduced me to a book called *How To Be Wildly Wealthy FAST* by Sandy Forster. The book wasn't just about creating mad wealth, but it introduced many techniques aligned with the Law of Attraction and so were transferable to any area of my life at that time. I soaked up the knowledge in this book quickly and set about testing out some of the techniques. At that time, I was living in London and was working as a probation officer, which was a job I loved; however, having grown up in the UK, I was really getting over the weather, the drabness, and the concrete jungle, that is London. I love London, but I was really starting to dislike it at that point and longed to be somewhere sunny, with beautiful beaches and palm trees.

I knew that I wanted the move to Australia to be permanent, to raise a family there, and to have a better quality of life, a lifestyle, and one that I couldn't see myself having in the UK. While it was tempting (*So* tempting!) to jack it all in, get a working holiday visa, and head straight to Australia, I wanted to ensure I had enough skills and enough money to set me up well there and to ensure I could get permanent residency. So at that time, I wanted about four years of experience in probation and to start building some adequate savings.

I used the tips in Sandy's book to begin manifesting some extra cash, as well as *seeing* myself as living in Australia, and I was talking about it non-stop.

Working in probation, I had a fixed salary. However, I had also been teaching Reiki and doing Reiki treatments for a few years, and this was an additional source of income for me. So what I focused on was bringing in some extra cash to be able to get a nice amount of savings going.

I used a combination of things to make this happen. First, I set a strong intention that I was *definitely* moving to Australia and nothing in the universe would stop me from achieving that dream. My desire was insanely strong. I started doing some positive affirmations and literally flooded my head with them. When I first started doing affirmations, it was February. I set a *smart* goal (specific, measureable, achievable, realistic, and time-framed) to bring in an additional £300 per week from my Reiki business, Phoenix Transformation. I could do this by giving Reiki treatments after work and by teaching Reiki. I planned to achieve this by the end of March. So about midway through February, I began relentlessly affirming to myself, 'I am *so* happy and grateful that I now attract at least £300 per week profit into my business, on top of my current salary.' I included the emotions of being happy and grateful, as putting feelings and really *feeling* them when doing your affirmations magnetises your goals towards you even faster, so does gratitude.

I said 'at least' so that I didn't cap it, and the universe could provide *even more* than that to me because I didn't put a limit on it.

So I said this affirmation to myself over and over and over and over again – it was literally the only thing I allowed myself to think! I then also took inspired action – by talking to potential clients, putting an ad on Gum tree, and so on. You can't just sit back and dream, not take any action, and expect things to fall into your lap. I am a massive action person. Within *one week*, I had £1,200 worth of bookings for March which averages out at £300 a week! Literally only one week of doing these affirmations and I achieved the goal. I was stunned at this and so I upped the goal to manifest £400 a week instead and did that affirmation for the last week of February. As a result, by the end of February, I had £1,600 worth of bookings for March, which was exactly what I brought in that month. For me that was a lot of money to be bringing in on the side of my full-time job, considering I had a limited amount of time in the week to actually bring in that additional income.

This just got me absolutely hooked on the Law of Attraction, and I have used so many other processes since then. It's so fun to manifest what you want! Two years later, I achieved my dream of moving to Australia and I'm just going through my permanent residency now. I manifested my gorgeous man one day after writing out my cosmic wish list for the type of relationship I wanted to attract. I moved to Perth where I am surrounded by beautiful endless stretches of beach, palm trees, and the best weather. Last year, I even manifested a $10,000 lottery win! I also ended up doing my life coach training through Sandy Forster's Inspired Spirit Coaching Academy and am now a certified Law of Attraction coach. I truly am living the life of my dreams, and every day I wake up so grateful and excited for what else I will manifest. Thank you, universe!

About Coach Carly

Carly Evans is the creator of Coach Carly and Phoenix Transformation. Carly has worked with people across the globe from all walks of life since 2006, helping them to realise and reach their full potential through powerful transformational coaching processes using principles embedded in Universal Laws such as the Law of Attraction and Law of Manifestation. Carly is a contributing author in the bestselling Adventures in Manifesting series in a book titled *Soulful Relationships*.

Carly Evans
www.coachcarly.com.
carlyevans@ruah.com.au

Losing Weight and Martial Arts LOA Style

Desire: Lose Weight and Get Fit
Time Frame: Three and a Half Years

After a few years of being slightly overweight, having trouble bending over to do up shoe laces, getting puffed easily when walking up stairs, and also being sick of looking at my bulges in photos, I yearned to be slim and trim.

One day, I imagined myself being nice and slim, and the feeling I got when I did this excited me, so I began to imagine this more and more. I would picture myself looking and feeling sexy in a sleeveless figure-hugging dress which came down to just above my knees. In this vision, my hair was also looking healthy and beautiful to match my nice new figure. This image of me would come to my mind quite often for a month or so.

Then one day, out of the blue, I was sitting in front of a cake and about to have a piece and I realised I ate way too many sugary foods and I was sick of it. So I decided on the spot to do away with this type of food. Surprisingly, I found it quite easy to resist cakes and similar foods. I ended up losing quite a few kilos and started looking better. The vision that I had was starting to come true; however, about six months later, I found myself starting to eat all these sweet foods again. I tried hard to resist, but I couldn't, and it started to become a real problem for me. My desire for losing weight was still within me, and the universe was aware of this because I was eventually introduced to a group of people who were using spiritual principles to overcome their food problems. I started attending their meetings and realised it was exactly what I needed. I ended up losing more weight but also started to have peace of mind as I overcame my emotional difficulties by loving and accepting myself and others.

After becoming trim, taut, and terrific, I was ready for new adventures. I always wanted to learn self-defence and also wanted my five-year-old daughter to learn some defence tactics as well. I put my desire out to the universe, but I didn't really make much of an effort to look for a class because I didn't think I could find a class that would be suitable because of where I lived. I lived out of town and thought I would have to do classes in town which I didn't want to do. I also thought I would have to do a separate class to my daughter as well and I thought the whole thing would be too much of a hassle. I was trying very much to keep my life simple. But of course, I still had the desire within me. I believe that true desires never leave you.

Anyway, lo and behold, one day, my daughter came home from school with the school newsletter which had an advertisement about a martial arts class being held not far from where we lived. So I rang the instructor's number and booked my daughter in. I thought the class would only be for children and asked if they had any classes for adults, and he told me the class was for both kids and adults. The universe responded exactly to my desire. I even had a female instructor who was perfect for me. I didn't know how it was all going to happen, but the universe did. These classes had only been going for about a few weeks prior, which was probably the same time my desire had been born.

So my daughter and I toddled off to our first class. I was so nervous the whole time, I kept giggling, but I did keep going back.

So there I was thirty-five years old learning martial arts. I had never done anything like it before, and I was not very fit or flexible either. Within my first year of doing the sport I loved, I was learning, and I enjoyed watching the higher ranks perform. However, I had lots of problems. It took me ages to pick up each technique, and I was very slow at sparring. I progressed very slowly and was very self-conscious in the classes, and my self-doubt kept telling me to give up. Fortunately, my determination kept me going.

The first thing I had to do was change my attitude. I had to become aware of the thoughts that were running through my mind which were things like 'I can't do this, I'll never be any good, I'm hopeless, and I'm kidding myself'. As soon as I realised this, I changed my self-talk to 'I can do this.' Things then began to change. My performance got better.

After this, I decided to use the Law of Attraction process of visualisation to get even better. I would imagine myself doing flying sidekicks and would feel the adrenaline rush through my body as I was flying through the air. I would actually feel this in my body as I was visualising. I would imagine myself doing board breaks. I would visualise feeling my foot going through the board as it broke and hearing the crack of the board. And I imagined myself sparring really well also.

After a few weeks of doing this visualisation process, something just clicked for me, and I started to get better and began to enjoy the class a lot more as well. My instructor even came up to me after a class and said, 'I have noticed a big change in you lately. It all seems to be working out for you. Well done!' I knew in my heart it was because I had been doing the visualisation.

The main factor in this manifestation was that the visualisation was fuelled with excitement. I didn't actually sit down every day at a certain time and visualise in a certain way for a certain amount of time; it wasn't structured. I don't do that well with structure. If I do any Law of Attraction process which feels like a chore, it won't work. I practiced the process nearly every day only for about a minute whenever I felt like it, even when I was driving my car, but the excitement I was feeling made the visualisation process more powerful. I believe this to be the key to manifesting using visualisation. It has to be mixed with excitement.

Carmel Heale
Law of Attraction coach
www.wealthbecomesme.com

A SEA CHANGE

Desire: Buying a Beach House
Time Frame: Three Years

Ask and the universe lines it up, and then all you have to do is allow it in.
Ask

It was early January 2009, and we reluctantly left the beachfront unit we'd been renting for our week of sand, sea, and sun on the Sunshine Coast and decided it would be nice to drive along with the ocean in view for a little bit longer on the trip back to Brisbane.

As we drove along the beachfront, there was a suburb away from where we holidayed. We noticed how quiet and peaceful and inviting the neighbourhood seemed. It was less touristy and more suburban beachfront, and as we drove, I remember thinking how amazing it would be to live there. I felt the desire quite strongly. So there was my vibrational 'ask', and I said to my husband, 'I wonder what it would take to live here in one of these houses close to the beach.' I really only asked once, but it felt very strong in vibration I remember how free, vibrant, and inspiring it felt driving along that road with the ocean on our left and houses on our right and the intensity of being open to possibility. In that moment, it felt outside of our reality and just seemed to be a nice dream but neither of us completely rejected the idea.

The Universe Lines it Up

We moved back into our usual routine once we returned to Brisbane, but we did have a decision to make and that was which school we would send our son to next year. We had been contemplating our options for some time and were a bit lost in the options available, so I meditated and asked that the divine right path would open up to us. Suddenly, one morning, as I was unpacking the dishwasher, the idea popped into my head. What about moving to the Sunshine Coast? It matched the energy of our drive along the beach. We worked from home. There really was nothing keeping us in Brisbane. We applied to our chosen school on the Coast, and by May, we'd received an offer for our son to attend from 2010. The final months of the year was spent looking at houses to rent somewhere near the school, which wasn't near the beach, and it wasn't inspiring. We missed some because they rented too quickly and rejected others because they weren't quite right.

Again I started meditating and asked that the divine right home for us would be presented to us. Then as the year came to a close, we were approached by a Mum whose son went to the same preschool as our son. She was also moving to the Sunshine Coast as well and had also been looking for somewhere to rent and had secured a place near the beach that had not been listed for rent yet as it was a break lease. She now needed to opt out because the current tenant had changed the exit date. We were more flexible in our ability to take over the lease from the current tenant. At this Mum's insistence, we went and looked at the property. It was in the very area we had driven through in January, but we just hadn't considered this as an option and certainly there had been no suitable houses listed publicly for rent, but the universe has ways of making things happen. We applied, were accepted, and moved in the first week of January 2010.

Allow

Not knowing what it would really be like to live at the beach, renting enabled us to 'dip our toe' in so to speak and 'test drive' the suburb before we committed to buying anything. Straight away, we fell in love with the beach and the neighbourhood and of course the house and felt perpetually grateful that we'd been guided to it. We quickly felt the need to own it rather than rent it, but we heard how much the owner had paid for the house and felt sure we'd never be able to afford to own it ourselves. That was a belief that took us some abundance work to shift, including a lot of visualising and energetic clearing with Access Consciousness tools around money to go beyond the limiting beliefs. By 2012, we had definitely experienced a change in consciousness around money, and as a result of this and a drop in the housing market, the owner agreed to sell the house to us at a price that we agreed too. So by the end of 2012, we were the owners of our house near the beach and still continue to be in awe and appreciation of the unfolding.

One afternoon, after we'd purchased our 'beach house' and three years after moving to the Coast, we were walking along the beach, and as we walked past another couple, we heard the woman comment about how nice it would be to live here. That was her 'asking.' I'm sure in that moment, the universe lined it up. And the man said, 'Don't be ridiculous,' and proceeded to list work, money, living in reality, and whatever else as legitimate reasons why they couldn't live here. My husband and I just smiled at each other knowing it is possible, if you're willing to allow it. It just might take them a while.

Jillian Jones
www.JillianJones.com

JOB OF A LIFETIME

Desire: Prestigious Art Teaching Position
Time Frame: Six Months

Madeline wanted a very specific job in a specific institution. Her desire was strong and clear. She was given a book called *Creative Visualization* by Shakti Gawain while she was a casual teacher at that same institution. She felt she had no security since the pay was poor and the money was erratic because it was a casual work.

That created the desire for this particular job since it would give her both the stability and the consistent money with great superannuation and sick days.

Madeline really took to this book and decided to try out this visualising technique. Being highly visual as an artistic person, it came quite naturally to her.

What she did first was she got clear about what she wanted. That part was easy; she wanted a full-time, high-profile position in a particular institution that was located in a specific place, where she already had the privilege of working casually.

Next, she created a scene, which she visualised every night. The scene was being congratulated by the people she worked with. In the scene, they said to her, 'Congratulations for getting the job!' and they shook her hand. There were four people in that scene. She was standing in the administration building. There was a statue of Venus in that location.

Madeline also would go and visit that building and say to herself as she was there, 'I belong here,' feeling as if she already did.

At the time, she was working one day a week teaching, one day doing administration, and two days studying.

When she was offered the job six months later, the scene she had created had played itself out just like she had visualised it. The four people she knew that had been the people in her visualisation said those words to her, 'Congratulations for getting the job!' and they shook her hand. The only difference was there were five people there when it really happened.

Madeline had the pleasure of that job for ten years, and it gave her the three things she really wanted: 1) security, 2) increase in money, and 3) improved self-esteem.

PICKLES AND COLOMBIAN BUTTERFLEAS

Desire: Soulmate
Time Frame: Four Months

For those of you who do not know me and to those of you who do not fully understand the Law of Attraction, what you're about to read may seem quite strange. In fact, you might think that I've been Pixie-led or run away with the Faeries. For those of you who know me and for those of you who believe in magic and the Law of Attraction, everything you're about to read will make perfect sense.

Here is one of my stories, my desires, and some of my mantras which I would say on a daily basis repeating them constantly, especially while walking my dog on the bush track on our way to the beach for a swim. Constantly, I would be speaking to the universe, my Guardian Angels, Pacha Mama, Inti, the Faeries, everyone who would be able to help align the stars and allow my desires to become reality with harm to none and so it is. When Agnes asked if I would write this story for her second book, I was overjoyed with excitement! I was excited for allowing my story to be in Agnes's second book along with the other Law of Attraction stories for everyone to read. I hope to inspire you to continue believing, continue dreaming, continue believing in your desires, and turn them into reality.

For years, I had desired a relationship with a man from South America and to have children which grow up learning about two different cultures, languages, and having the opportunity to work and travel in two different countries. Three years ago, I told my mother that she would have grandchildren that would grow up speaking Spanish. She laughed at the time . . . but since August 2013, my mother started to believe me!

My lovely, beautiful, crazy, Flamenco-dancing friend Carla, whom I have known for twenty-one years, introduced me to Agnes a few years ago. How grateful I am for this introduction and to now be able to call Agnes a very dear friend. Agnes is a beautiful, crazy French woman who loves to dance. Carla and Agnes

38

are part of 'My Flock.' We are all equally crazy, understand one another, laugh hysterically, and love music and dance. We all started going to Salsa Clubs to dance, have a spectacular night out with the girls, and see who we could find . . . as all single women (and men) do! Walking into the clubs hearing the salsa music playing as loud as it was possible would start my feet tapping, send shivers down my spine, and place an instant smile on my face. I love this music, the rhythm, the dance, the feeling it gives me, and instant happiness. It is a kind of meditation for me! During these hilarious night outs with my lovely friends, it was confirmed to me that I would have to find a man who enjoyed dancing.

Agnes would talk and teach Carla and me about the Law of Attraction. To be honest, at first, I was a little sceptical about everything. However, Agnes would continue to talk about things which she had changed in her life and tell stories of her friends who had also changed things in their lives or bought cars and houses which they had been dreaming about or desiring, for some time. I began organising my mantras and religiously started repeating them. Agnes would say, 'Repeat your mantras while you're travelling in the bus, while you're out walking, when you're collecting frangipanis, while doing the dishes, while in the shower . . . *anywhere*!' I would write my mantras on hand cards and Blu-tack them to my bedroom walls, taking old mantras down, rewriting them, and putting new ones up. I still do this and have mantras stuck to my walls.

After a conversation with Agnes one evening in early 2013 and having had enough of constantly attracting travelling men into my life and yes, those men were all from South America, I decided to concentrate on what truly I desired in a man with whom I could have a relationship with. I will never forget what Agnes answered my question with, 'Sarah, stop telling the universe what you don't want! It's that simple. Just tell the universe what you do want!' This comment was followed by Agnes's most beautiful laugh which I adore. So that is exactly what I did. I stopped asking for what I didn't want and started asking for what I desired.

When talking to my beautiful sister, Wiz, one day about my desires and wishes in regards to attracting and meeting the man of my dreams, there was one comment from Wiz which stuck in my mind and changed many thoughts and mantras along the way. What Wiz said was simple. 'So, why Brazilian? Why not a man from South America? There are so many other countries and you've been to Mexico, Peru, Bolivia, and Ecuador, why not a man from one of those countries or Argentina or Colombia or just somewhere else!' So my mantras changed. 'South American' was added to some, Spanish-speaking was added, and then came the salsa-dancing mantras. Then it was 'South American, Spanish-speaking, and Salsa dancing'. Always remember that your first mantra will never be the one that you stick with. You will change them, add details, and so on which is totally fine, and there are no rules to writing your own mantras!

Here is a collection of mantras as examples of what I was sending out to the universe and the dates at which these mantras were being said.

6.4.13

'Would like to plan and save for a holiday in a tropical, Spanish-speaking country, to learn Spanish, explore, make new friends, and travel.'

26.5.13

'I now attract the best relationship I've ever had.'

'I now attract an amazing, loving, caring, passionate relationship with a man who loves me and is true to me.'

'Wouldn't it be nice to have a relationship with a man who is loving, caring, passionate, great fun to be with, loves to salsa and speaks Spanish, is true to me, loves me and makes my heart smile? This relationship leads to us getting married to one another and having children.'

23.7.13

'I desire to have an amazing, loving, caring, passionate relationship with a gorgeous South American, Spanish-speaking, and salsa-dancing man who loves and respects me.'

25.8.13

'I am happy and grateful now that I have a wonderful relationship with a gorgeous Spanish-speaking, salsa-dancing, loving, caring, passionate man who loves and respects me.'

'I will meet and have an amazing relationship with a gorgeous South American, Spanish-speaking, salsa-dancing, loving, caring, passionate man who is respectful towards me, friendly, easy-going. This gorgeous, passionate man is out there looking for me, as I am looking for him. When we see each other, we will know that we are to be together.'

'I am loved. I am respected. I am happy. I am very grateful to have the most wonderful relationship with a gorgeous, passionate, loving, caring, salsa-dancing, Spanish-speaking man who is respectful and loves me. He is loved. He is respected. He is happy. We are happy together. This man of my dreams does exist. He is out there in the universe looking for me, and when the time is right for both of us, the universe will come together and help us find and meet each other. We will find each other.'

31.8.13

'I have a wonderful, loving, caring, passionate, respectful relationship with a Spanish-speaking, gorgeous, salsa-dancing man who loves and respects me.'

Be patient with your mantras and the universe. The universe delivers your desires when she knows you are ready to accept them. Your desires may appear to you as glimpses prior to revealing themselves completely. I was given glimpses of 'The Colombian' prior to our actual introduction when we were at the Cuban Place in late August; our relationship started in early September.

While Agnes, Carla, and I were out at The Cuban Place in July/August 2013, we danced with many different men as is the case when out salsa dancing. However, there was one man which we all remembered and enjoyed dancing with, the cheeky curly haired Colombian. Over the course of a few weeks, we all danced with 'The Colombian' – an amazing dancer and a very patient man, teaching me the correct Colombian salsa steps. On 24 August 2013, Agnes was dancing with Edisson for hours. Carla and I watched on while we weren't dancing as we were mesmerised by his rhythm. At one stage, Agnes came over to us and said, 'I've found this amazing dancer, and I shall be dancing with him tonight if you need me.' Then off she went into the crowd and was lost in dance. Carla and I giggled and knew we wouldn't see Agnes for a while. As the night turned into the early hours of the morning, Agnes came over to me holding Edisson's hand. 'Sarah, you must dance with this man. He is a great dancer. Edisson, this is my friend Sarah. Dance together.' As Agnes said these words, she put my hand into Edisson's and held both our hands for a moment. This was just how I had imagined I would meet a gorgeous man . . . which might have had something to do with the book *Solomon's Song* by Sarah de Carvehlo which I'd recently read. Edisson and I then spent the remainder of the evening together dancing and gazing into each other's eyes as it were.

Two weeks went by. Agnes, Carla, and I decided to go salsa dancing at Cruise Bar on Thursday. As I walked to the bus stop, I spoke to the universe the following:

'Universe, I realise for the past few months I've been sending out very mixed and confusing messages about a certain desire I have in regards to men. Yes, I'd like to meet a gorgeous man whom I can have fun with; however, what I really desire is a wonderful relationship with a gorgeous Spanish-speaking, salsa-dancing, passionate, easy-going, friendly, loving, caring man. I desire a relationship which is loving, caring, passionate, and respectful with a man who loves and respects me. Please, tonight, introduce me to that man.'

Carla and I had a delicious dinner. As we walked closer to the Cruise Bar, my instincts were telling me that 'The Colombian' was there. 'Carla, I have a really strange feeling that "The Colombian" is at the Cruise Bar. I have butterflies in my stomach and I haven't eaten any caterpillars today.' Both of us laughed hysterically and made our way to the Cruise Bar for some salsa with Agnes. It was a gorgeous night. Not a cloud to be seen in a star-lit sky with the best view of Sydney Harbour.

Within five minutes of arriving at the Cruise Bar, Carla spotted 'The Colombian'. Agnes found us after just having had a dance and a chat with 'The Colombian.'

I was completely confused as my heart was telling me to give this gorgeous, Spanish-speaking, salsa-dancing man a chance. My instincts were telling me he was older than he had originally said. Agnes danced with 'The Colombian' as Carla tried to convince me that he wouldn't talk to me again or ask me to dance because I hadn't pursued him since our last meeting due to the confusion with age. However, within seconds of Carla finishing that sentence, 'The Colombian' was standing in front of me smiling ever so cheekily asking me to dance.

'The Colombian' looked absolutely gorgeous wearing jeans and a black T-shirt and not having shaved for a few days. All I wanted to do was kiss him! Gorgeous, curly headed Colombian man, an amazing dancer, was standing in front of me, holding my hand with a cheeky smile. My heart was smiling. What was a girl to do?

Exactly what I had asked the universe for was standing in front of me. The universe had ensured that we would both meet each other again and that night at the Cruise Bar was the night we would start our relationship. We spent the entire night together, dancing, laughing, chatting to our friends, and having an amazing night together. When I saw 'The Colombian' again that night, I knew this man would be in my life for a very long time, and this man was the man I had been searching for. Edisson is my *soulmate*. Edisson is the man who will forever make my heart smile.

Thinking about that night, I can close my eyes and see everything replay itself exactly as it happened. Edisson and I speak of the night we first met, and both of us are very grateful to Agnes for introducing us by placing our hands in one another's, suggesting we dance with one another all those months ago!

Edisson is exactly what I had been searching for in a man, a gorgeous, passionate, loving, caring, cheeky, salsa-dancing, and Spanish-speaking man. How lucky that our paths had crossed at The Cuban! How grateful I am that Agnes met Edisson on the dance floor, that Agnes then introduced the two of us, and that Edisson chose to travel to Australia. Extremely grateful that the universe heard my desires over the months of constantly repeating the mantra and listened to me as I walked to the bus stop that night. I am grateful and ever so happy my desires were turned into reality and I had the support of my inspirational friends, the universe, Pacha Mama, Inti, the Faeries, and my Guardian Angels to assist me along the journey.

This mantra made me smile when I reread it and is one of many which proves that when you believe in your desires, they do come true! I wrote this particular mantra in my journal on 6 April 2013. 'Would like to be in a loving, caring, honest, trustworthy, passionate, happy relationship with a gorgeous Spanish-speaking, salsa-dancing man before the end of October 2013 which will lead to marriage and children'. Edisson and I had been together for two months by the end of October 2013.

Another mantra I had been saying during the same time I was saying the mantras already mentioned earlier was dated on 26 May 2013. 'Wouldn't it be nice to travel to a Spanish-speaking country in 2014?' Having desired to go on a holiday to a Spanish-speaking country for some time, desiring to venture back to South America after travelling through Ecuador, Peru, Bolivia, and Mexico over ten years ago, to explore even more of that beautiful part of the world, you can imagine my excitement when Edisson asked if I would like to join him on a holiday to Colombia to meet his family! Edisson and I spent seven wonderful weeks travelling around Colombia, setting off at the end of March 2014. I spent time in Cartagena with his mother, sister, and nephew. Edisson and I also travelled to Bogota, Santa Marta, and his family's home town, which is absolutely beautiful, spending time with his family and friends. Edisson's family and friends are extremely friendly, welcoming, lovely, happy bunch of people. Everyone welcomed me warmly, and even though there was a language barrier, we all had a wonderful time laughing and getting to know one another. Both Edisson and I are very much looking forward to travelling back to Colombia in the years to come, eventually travelling with our children and living in Colombia for a while. I have vowed to Edisson to be able to speak Spanish fluently prior to our next Colombian adventure!

Excerpt from my journal dated 22 October 2013 titled *The Butterflea effect!'*

Yes, butterflea, no that's not a typo and for those of you who know, will have a giggle, just as Edisson and I did over twelve months ago!

> Extremely grateful to have Carla and Agnes as my amazing, lovely friends. Grateful the three of us share the love of dance and go salsa dancing together, enjoying the music and meeting new people. Grateful for Carla for introducing Agnes to me. Grateful to Agnes for introducing me to the world of Law of Attraction and changing my thoughts and way of thinking. Grateful to Agnes for finding Edisson on the dance floor that night we went to The Cuban Place and telling me, 'Sarah, you must dance with this man!' Grateful to the universe to allow Edisson and me to meet. Grateful that Edisson decided he wanted to travel to Sydney. Grateful to Carla and Agnes for going out that night, grateful to Carla for suggesting we go to the Cruise Bar on that Thursday for salsa. Grateful for speaking with the universe on my way to the bus stop and setting my desires straight. Grateful that Edisson and his friends decided to go to The Cuban Place and then to Cruise Bar on the same nights we ventured there, so we were all able to meet one another, dance with each other and become friends.

It took me a little while to figure out my exact desires and organise my messages to the universe, but with Agnes's help, support, love, and laughter, I eventually figured it all out. Edisson and I have been together since that night at the Cruise Bar. This year, we spent seven weeks travelling around Colombia with his family and friends. We have moved in together and speak regularly about our children we plan to have. Never have I been so completely in love and happy with a man. Every time I think about Edisson, I smile. Each time I look at Edisson, I fall in love with him again and again and again. Edisson certainly makes my heart smile and has shown me what true love really is.

There is a quote which states 'One day someone will walk into your life and make you realize why it never worked out with anyone else.' Edisson is my someone. He is my true love, my soulmate, my friend, my lover, my salsa-dancing,

Spanish-speaking, gorgeous, passionate, loving, caring man who makes my heart smile. Thank you! Thank you! Thank you!

Invest in your dreams and desires, as only you are able to turn them into reality with positive thoughts and actions. Be grateful. Give thanks to everyone who assists you on your journey and not just after your desires have become reality. Give thanks every day, every time you say your mantras. I found it best to speak to 'My Helpers' while I was out in the sunshine, in the park, at the beach, in the bush. This is where I find my peace and relaxation. My mantras became a kind of meditation for me. A meditation in improving my life and allowing myself to gain access to everything I desired to change and so it is with harm to none.

There is magic in the world. One must open your eyes to it and believe!

Appreciation. Gratefulness. Happiness. Love. Passion. Friends. Laughter. Dance. Luck. Sunshine. Chance. Belief. Magic.

It is truly amazing how everything works in this universe, the butterflea effect and how the universe works in very mysterious ways!

Remember: always be grateful, always give thanks, always appreciate, always allow yourself to see the magic, always smile and be happy!

Never settle for anything less than butterfleas!

UNSEEN FRIEND

Desire: To do Jingles on the Radio
Time Frame: Ten Years

Dominique is my creative soulmate. We met at Sydney College of Advanced Education at the Oatley Campus in Sydney, Australia, in 1987. We were both studying there doing a Diploma in Performing Arts. We were the final batch of students in Australia to get free education, because from the following year, even if you were half way through a degree, you had to start paying the fees; hence, we were really lucky. We had heaps of fun learning drama and dance at a time where legwarmers and lycra were hot fashion items, and we were sure Michael Jackson was the second coming.

Dominique is an oddonite. She really comes from Planet Odd. She is one of the people that make the world a better place, simply by how she views the world and people. She thinks weird is normal, and that is why I love her so much.

So the jingle story, for those of you that don't know what a jingle is, it's when you hear on the radio an ad, and there is singing with catchy lines in it to back up the product being advertised.

Dom was one of seven children, and they all went to church growing up. All the children sang in church, so singing was a natural part of life in the Smiths' household in the 1960s and 1970s, Vaughntrap style. Dom went on to sing at weddings and funerals and still does to this day. She said to me the other day, 'It's strange I have to wait for someone to die to get work.'

The dates of this story are a bit hazy; however, in the early 2000s, Dom was living in London due to her husband's work, and she and a friend both got pregnant at the same time and were attending pre-natal classes together. This friend of her did voice-overs (a piece of narration in a film or broadcast not accompanied by an image of the speaker), and Dom mentioned to her, her desire to do jingles. Her friend tried to put her off by telling her how hard it was to get into and how not many people succeeded. Dom confidently thought to herself, 'You haven't heard me sing. I reckon I can do that hands down, I am as good as anyone.'

I want to emphasise here Dom is far from arrogant. She had been singing for a long time and really believes in herself which from the Law of Attraction point of view is majorly important. Belief is key in manifesting anything; it's the 'Open Sesame.'

After that, her friend had her child and they lost contact. Dom relocated back to Sydney due to her husband's work. She crossed paths with a guy she had sung and done an entertainment show with years ago. At this timely encounter, he was working for 2GB radio, and she mentioned to him that she wanted to do jingles. He put her on the books, and she was extremely excited and grateful for this step closer to her dream. She told me that she just kept thinking, 'I want to be writing the jingles and singing the jingles too.' She felt she could easily do it given the opportunity.

Dom didn't end up working for 2GB, but this isn't the end of the story. She continued to sing at funerals through word of mouth, and one day, she got a call from a best friend from school who was dying. Anna made her promise on her deathbed to keep singing and said to her, 'I want you to be a rock star. You will be on radio.' Anna made Dom promise that she would never stop singing.

Anna was a singer and songwriter, and when they were at school, they sealed their friendship with a ritual of cutting their fingers and smearing their blood together. Dom, through tears of remembrance, told me they had become blood sisters.

So back to 'I want to do jingles,' in the pool in London. Dom thought to herself, 'How does one get there? They had to have started somehow.'

Years later, Dom was asked to sing at Anna's dad's funeral. While in the shower, she had this strong feeling that something big was going to happen that day. She squashed the feeling and off she went to sing for her best friend's dad. They wanted to pay her, and she declined. She wanted to do it for Anna, for love.

After the funeral, Anna's sister's best friend approached her and said, 'What are you doing with that voice?' She was the marketing manager for Travel World. Dom told her she wanted to do jingles. She asked Dom to write and sing a jingle for them! Then she freaked out – How do I write a jingle? How much do I charge? Dom was extremely fortunate to know the exact people to ask those questions to, and she found out to lease the jingle and not sell it outright to them. This was the advice from a lawyer friend. Another friend who was in the industry helped her sift through all the industry jargon, and with the influence of the Andrew's sisters (singers in the 1960s), Dom wrote a brilliant jingle.

On 17 June 2010, on Anna's birthday, the signed contract was returned. Dom leased the jingle for $25,000 a year and was paid in advance in November since they had to spend the money allocated in that year's budget. The jingle ran for three years at $25,000 a year, and this year 2014, Dom has five different jingles currently running on a major station ABC for kids.

Creatives can make money, without a doubt, but the belief has to precede the manifestation.

Currently, Dominique is singing for funerals, doing jingles, and working on something for kids, but I can't tell you what it is because it hasn't hatched yet. Dominique can be contacted via her website.

Dominique English
Dominique.com.au

CREATIVELY $100K

Desire: $100,000 Per Year
Time Frame: Five Years

'Creative people don't make money,' that was my belief for many years. No one in my extended family had done well creatively, and I didn't know anyone personally that had.

I knew so many creative people though that had hobbies or tried to make money doing what they loved, but they had other jobs on the side to support what they really loved to do.

Then I met a woman in the Blue Mountains. She had a candle shop that was doing extremely well, and she was an artist and sold her paintings within her own store. She was one of the first people I had ever met that broke that belief for me. Twelve years later, that shop is still going strong and she is still doing well. Interestingly, she taught me indirectly about the Law of Attraction by watching her do things and listening to how she talked and thought.

I ended up working for her and learned a lot about creativity, money, and attraction in general.

I then moved to the central coast and got a job working in a retail store. It was fun, but I preferred doing the displays to doing the selling. I remember thinking, 'I would love to do just this fun part,' and decided to see if that was possible. I looked around for visual merchandising jobs but never seemed to get anywhere with the applying or the interviews. I still didn't believe that it was possible to have that great of a job.

I asked my employer at the time for a transfer to Sydney, which was about an hour and a half away, and at the time, he didn't have anything, but not too long after, I think it was about six months I got a transfer to the city which meant it was easier to find those kind of positions. While I was in that job, I would stand behind the counter and write for half an hour what I currently loved about that job. I really felt trapped, suffocated, and really wanted to leave, but I knew I had to change how I felt if I was going to attract anything better. I religiously did this list every day; I was often alone with no one in the store, so it was easy.

There was another home wares store two doors down. This crazy, fun guy I got to meet used to do their displays in the window. He was a real certified organic nut. He was six foot and had a happy ridiculous energy, and I instantly liked him. He would often stop and chat. He was a massive extrovert, and he knew everyone around there, or seemed to, since I always saw him chatting and laughing with people. I remember thinking, 'Wow, I would love to do what he does!'

So one day, Craig came to see me and said, 'Do you want to get out of here?' The magic sentence of the century. I told him I did, and he referred me on to a client of his, George, who had a large shop at a shopping centre ten minutes down the road. He said to me, 'Before you go, think about what you want because George will ask you.' Well . . . wow, I was gobsmacked! I thought about what I wanted, and it was the following:

1. Four days a week
2. No weekends
3. Doing the displays
4. Doing the ordering of the home wares
5. Increasing my income
6. Working with like-minded people
7. Get on wonderfully with my boss

So I went to see George, and we had a great meeting, and I received everything on that list (except doing the ordering until about eight months later, and flying to Melbourne to do the trade fairs ordering once a year and do the Sydney trade fairs twice a year too).

I loved working there. I loved the girls and I loved doing the displays and I loved George too. It was wonderful. Three years later, the shopping centre went under massive renovation, and it was a mess. Customers really dropped off so badly, in fact, that George had to shut the shop. He did, however, relocate us to a shop that was much smaller and sold only kitchen things. I was depressed, as I was not a fan of selling pots and pans, and my position of doing displays, buying, and being creative virtually disappeared. I did understand George's position and so did the rest of the staff, so we all moved to the new cooking store, and I made a decision to focus my way out of there, even before we moved there since we had over a month to know it was going to happen.

At the new location, I felt trapped again. It was in a dense-populated spot, and I felt suffocated and started to feel minor panic attacks being trapped in one small room with no creative things to do. Waaaaahhhh, poor me!

So I started to do this:

As I walked to work, I would say to myself, 'Oh, I won't be doing this walk from the car to work anymore shortly, so I won't be seeing this lovely house any more or that beautiful tree or that lovely flower garden.' I started to say good-bye to that neighbourhood as if I was leaving.

I also wrote a resignation letter stating I was moving on to another position and thanks for the time working with this lovely place that had helped me so much and would still continue to refer people to them. I folded it and popped it into my gratitude journal. I didn't give it to anyone nor tell anyone either.

I then told three people in the industry that I wanted to do only displays and if they heard of anything to let me know. Oddly, all three of them did. Janice, a representative of one of the companies I did the buying with, told me of a guy that had two stores and needed a Visual Merchandiser one day a week, so I started there and negotiated for myself double of what I had been used to. I continued to do the other job four days a week and added this fun day to my week. It increased my income by $1,600 a month, and I started to feel freer.

Then Matt a guy I knew also in the industry told me of some people that had three stores and they needed someone on and off. They too gave me some work and it was on a Sunday, so it didn't interfere with what I still had going on. Then Craig, the ridiculous crazy creative, got me the job that gave me enough work that I could leave my job! He asked me, 'How many days do you need to let go of your job totally?' We chatted and worked out the figures and hours, and I went off to see the husband and wife who today is a great source of inspiration to me and supply me with four days a week of 100 percent creative work. They allowed me to go freelance and be independent.

I said three affirmations during this last transition, and they were the key that opened the door to my freedom.

1. I work half the hours for twice the pay
2. I am free!
3. I now earn $10k a month from 1 November 2013 on an ongoing basis

I would say it while walking to the old job, when walking, while in the shower, and in the morning when waking, and any idle time really. I knew I had to leave George before November to give him time to find someone for Christmas. He was so kind to me I didn't want to leave him at peak time.

I left on 27 October 2013, and all the above statements are true except the first one. Often, it's a triple of what I had been earning the previous five years.

So I leave you with this: change your beliefs and then the outside follows, it's as simple as that.

Agnesvivarelli.com
Apersonofinterest.com.au
Apersonofinterest2014@gmail.com

WILL BE GOOD

Desire: Great Job in a Five-Star Hotel
Time Frame: Three Weeks

Pre-story:

As he was doing his three years formation at the hospitality middle school, Aurélien had to write applications for a trainee job. One practical year as a trainee was part of the requirements. The teachers gave the students a list of hotels in the region that they were to contact and recommended the students write five applications. Aurélien had a look at the list and decided to write only two, as only two hotels 'would suit him'. That was the moment I got nervous. I tried to explain to him that it would not be like this and that he should try to improve his chances to get somewhere by enlarging his choice. But while his colleagues were frenetically writing applications and betting on which hotel would give them the chance of an interview, Aurélien waited until the last minute to send his two applications. One of them was at a very good international hotel at the airport. Only two days later, he had his job interview with them and went back home. 'They will send me the job contract in the next week,' he said to me, to show me proof. 'Why are you always getting worried because of what can happen to me?' he asked.

The second hotel he had applied to responded a week later, offering him to come for an interview, but Aurélien's first choice contract with the international hotel was already signed. Of course, Aurélien seemed perfect for that kind of job: he spoke three languages, he's good-looking (I am his mum, so I can say that), and he likes being in contact with people and being seen. But he's also what you would call a minimalist when it comes to making an effort, which is the reason I've always been worrying, pushing, crossing fingers, etc.

The trainee year went fine. Aurélien was happy with the job and finished the practical year with a glowing reference report. He also managed to go through the last year of school and even passed the final exams, of course, without opening a book or worrying (that was my job and my duty) as the good marks in languages would do it. And they did.

The 'and-now-what-shall-I-do' question was not part of the plan, as Aurélien had to go to twenty-one weeks compulsory military service as is required by the French government.

The Story:

The army service was coming to its end. We were in March. Still one month to go. I already had nightmares, thinking about the time after it, imagining Aurélien enjoying my Hotel Mum, including laundry service and twenty-four hour restaurant, and me coming home in the evening with all my questions, 'Did you write applications today? Did you have any answer?' It would take two to three weeks and the atmosphere in our home would be unbearable.

One weekend, he was home in March. I allowed myself to ask him if he had some plans for the future. 'Mmmh . . . yeah . . . mmm . . . I shall think about finding a job.'

- 'But you *will have* to find a job!'

'Mmmh . . . yeah . . . no hurry. Sure I find something . . .'

'Do you have any plans? Do you know where you will apply?'

'Mmmhh . . . I will first need some holidays. Maybe two or three weeks. And then, I'll work at the X Hotel.'

The X (the hotel name has been omitted due to their policies) is one of the best hotels in Zurich. One of Aurélien's best mates did his practical year there and was happy with the job. And above all, the hotel is located at main station, which means you can get there directly with the train and don't need to worry about transportation. It's in the city centre, which means it's very convenient if you want to have a social life after work hours.

I tried to explain to Aurélien that it doesn't work like this. 'As a "twenty-year-old, fresh out-of-the-school young man without professional experience," you will more than likely send out around twenty applications and be *very* happy if you get one job interview and more than happy if you get a temporary job for a little while.'

'Anyway, I'll work there.'

Just in case, I, as worried Mum, went on the Internet and had a look at the hotel's website. It was written in big letters: NO STAFF VACANCIES. I said to Aurélien that although it's always good to have a goal, this one seemed to be quite compromised. He did not seem disappointed and left home to go back to the army. It was Sunday afternoon. I thought that Aurélien did not have any prepared and updated files for applications, so I decided to do the last thing I could do in that matter as a Mum. I sent an email to a friend of mine, who's working as a secretary, asking her if she could prepare a nice file with Aurélien's papers within a month or two.

In the evening, I suddenly remembered something. Although I usually don't keep contact with my former class students, I had made an exception the year before and accepted an invitation from one of them. That student was the X Hotel's director's son, and he had told me that he had worked with his dad as a quality manager. 'Why not?' I thought, 'I would try.' It was Sunday evening. I sent him an email, asking if Aurélien could send an application 'just in case'.

I had the answer on Monday. My student confirmed very politely that they had 'no staff vacancies', adding that if something would happen, he would let me know. I thanked him and sent a message to Aurélien: 'I tried. But you *will have* to change your plans. No jobs there.'

At the same time, I had a response from my secretary friend: 'No worries. Bring me the papers. I'll find some time to scan them in the next few weeks.'

Tuesday:

Just before noon, I got a new email from my former student: 'Dear Mrs Jacob, one of our receptionists surprisingly resigned yesterday. If your son wants to send his files, we'll have a look at his application. Kind Regards.' I replied: 'Thank you very much for the information. I'll contact Aurélien. Have a nice day.'

I text messaged my son, located with his soldiers' troop on the other side of the country:

'Do you want me to organise the application. I mean, "Are you ready to apply there?"'

Answer: 'Will be good.' (Please notice: not 'would be good', just 'Will be good'.)

Mail to my secretary friend: 'Sorry, but I need the files on Thursday. Can I bring you the papers tomorrow?'

Mail to my daughter: 'Can you please write a motivating cover letter for your brother and mail it to me tomorrow morning?'

To my German-speaking work colleague: 'Can you do me a favour and proofread a covering letter tomorrow?'

I spent Tuesday evening at home, sorting out all Aurélien's papers and trying to put a CV together, including finding an old picture which could still look as he actually did.

Wednesday: I met the secretary near her car in the morning before going to work and gave her a full sack of papers plus the CV. Then I had a look at the covering letter my daughter emailed and forwarded it to my colleague to proofread it. She did it that afternoon.

Thursday evening: The secretary had done wonders. When we met, she handed me some perfect prepared documents, everything sorted. At home, I searched Aurélien's passport to see how his signature would look like and reproduced it on the covering letter. I made some copies of all the documents and put them on Aurélien's bed for him to know what was sent, took a big envelope, and wrote the hotel address on it.

Friday morning: I brought the envelope to the post office and began to pray.

On Friday night, I was going away for the weekend with my daughter. Aurélien was spending the weekend alone at home. I left him a note: 'Have a look on your mobile and your emails, just in case the hotel is contacting you.'

Sunday night: I came back from Vienna and found Aurélien on the coach, half-asleep. 'Did you have a look at the papers we sent to the hotel? Is that OK for you?'

- 'Yeah . . . I'm working there next Sunday.'

'What?'

'They called me yesterday morning and asked if I could come for a job interview.'

'?'

'I was in bed, so I just had time to shower and take the train to be there at 1 p.m.'

(Mum's worry:) 'You found an ironed shirt in the cupboard?'

'Mmmmmh . . . No. My shoes (meaning the *only* one good pair of black shoes he has) were at the military barracks, so I could not wear a suit.'

'What? You went to a job interview in a five-star hotel in jeans and tennis shoes?'

'Mmmm . . . yes, but I had a clean T-shirt, and I told them I was coming straight from the army. They said it was OK.'

'!? And the interview?'

'Yeah, went well. They said my application was one of the nicest they never saw and that I'm qualified for the job. They are really happy I can speak French, and they said I should come next Sunday for a probation day.'

> The following Sunday, Aurélien went there, this time with black shoes, tie, ironed shirt (thanks, Mum!), and nice suit. He came back home very happy. 'I think they liked me.'

'Did you show them how you can speak the three languages?' (Aurélien's best argument for those kind of jobs is that he's trilingual.)

> 'Oh, yes. Just as I began, some French guest came to the reception. I spoke French to them and the reception chief's eyes nearly popped out. And there was also that other guest from Brisbane who asked me from which Australian state I was. I think the reception chief was quite impressed. The rest of the day was OK.'

A week after, my son had a new interview, this time with the human resource manager. The next Friday (last army weekend), he had an email from the hotel: 'We're really happy to welcome you in our team from 1st of May.'

Not only did Aurélien get the job, but he also could enjoy two weeks holiday after his military services. "Why should you always be worried and think that things will go bad?" As for people like him, everything always happens the way they want them to happen. You just need to have a goal and be true to yourself – and the whole world is on your side.

Mrs Jacob, Aurélien's mum

BEAK

Desire: To Connect with Nature
Time Frame: One Hour

I live in Sydney, Australia, and I love to go and explore and walk near my place. On this particular day, I set the intention before leaving home, 'I connect with nature.' My work is inside shopping centres, so getting outside on a day's off is really important to me.

I stuffed my headphones in my ears and off I went, 'Nico and Vinz' playing 'Am I Wrong.' I love this song so much I played it over and over eight times, and I was feeling the rush of the music. I so love how music affects me. You know I hatched in France, but my soul belongs to Africa. As a child growing up on Vancouver Island, I listened to a lot of Motown, R&B, and to me, Africans are the human musical notes and have the best music in the world.

So 'Nico and Vinz' 'Am I Wrong' eight times on a loop, and I was feeling exhilarated on my walk. These two guys are the only two that can get me to run up a hill, and I haven't run since about 1987.

I came around a corner, and there was this little walkway bridge over a marshy area, and as I came around, a Kookaburra was sitting on the bridge. I was walking fast, bopping to the music, and I nearly ran into him. Oddly, he wasn't fazed. I stopped abruptly . . . and his beak was inches away. I could see the hairs on it! Wow! He could have kissed my beak, for those of you that know me you know that I have one. I then saw his little pointy tongue come out, like he was licking his lips. So I stood there for what seemed like hours but was about ten minutes.

He recognised me, and I recognised him. As odd as that sounds, it's true. He smiled at me with his eyes. He was unafraid of me. I felt in tune with this feathered, grapefruit-sized friend with the hairs on his beak, and his odd little tongue.

I stood there for ages unmoving not wanting to break the moment. I felt such a rush I thought I was going to spontaneously combust, just my sneakers with the burnt laces left behind, earphones lying next to them. It got me wondering about spontaneous combustion. Is that what happens when there is a moment of

56

extreme exhilaration? The body can no longer hold it within the skin suit we wear! Hahahahaha random thought.

I *love you*, Mr Kookaburra, from Sydney, Australia. You are my twin soul. You reminded me to be unafraid of life today and how to feel connected without words. Thank you!

MY FRIEND, MY LOVER, MY SOULMATE

Desire: Soulmate
Time Frame: Three Weeks

In 2007, I was living in a lovely little apartment in an upmarket Brisbane suburb. I had been living by myself after leaving my marriage of twenty years. It had taken a lot of courage to do so, and I finally did it. I had been separated for around two years and was not that impressed with the dating scene. Now I wanted to find that someone special to settle down with.

I know it sounds so old-fashioned but that's just the type of girl I am, finding that someone to be with forever is the *dream*.

One night, I was sitting at home thinking about what I had experienced in the last two years within the dating scene, and yes, there were certainly some fun times but nothing truly meaningful or lasting. I came to the conclusion that dating is the pits and I no longer wanted to participate.

So I decided to pray to the universe. I honestly thought I had nothing to lose, and if anything, I was making it clear in my mind where I was heading from here. My prayer started off with, *If I was not meant to meet that someone special, someone that I would spend the rest of my life with, then that is OK. I will concentrate on myself, my children, my career and live the rest of my life feeling very happy and complete.*

I then decided to make a list of qualities I wanted in my life partner. I had heard putting it down on paper was like putting in an order (I still have this list today). I knew that this man was going to be someone very special, because as far as I was concerned, this would be it – the one, my friend, my lover, my soulmate. And if I couldn't find what I was looking for, I was prepared to go it alone if that was my journey and destiny.

A couple of weeks later, a girlfriend of mine invited me to a work function one Friday night. She mentioned she had someone for me to meet. At that point, I just thought, 'Oh that's nice,' and thought nothing more of it. So I met her at her work, had a glass of wine, and then we made our way to a small bar where there would be some salsa dancing – I love to dance, so thought that this would be a great night.

A group of us sat around a large table, talking, dancing, and generally being very merry and enjoying the night. I looked a couple of times at this man my friend had brought along, and once again thought not too much. He hadn't shown me much attention, so friends it would be!

Halfway through the night, my girlfriend came up to me and asked what I thought of him. I said straight away, 'He's not my type.' But as soon as I said these words, I could hear inside my mind, *You don't know your type. Wow,* could this be true?

I said to my girlfriend, 'You know what? I really shouldn't make that comment because I haven't really had a good long conversation with him. So I don't know what I think.'

An 'Ah Ha' moment for me!

During the evening, I had a couple of dances with this guy, and it was nice. At the end of the night, everyone was going in different directions to their homes; however, he was going my way and chivalrously offered to walk me to a cab in the city. On our way, he asked if I wanted to get a coffee, and I said that would be great. So we sat, ordered, and chatted for about an hour, really enjoying each other's company. We talked about our kids and work, nothing too serious, realising that we did have some things in common, kids and being previously married – no judgment here!

Once we left the cafe, he walked me to a cab rank where we exchanged business cards and said 'goodbye, lovely to meet you' and went our separate ways. It was nice to have good company and not feel the stress or the expectations of a date. So as you can see, it was not love at first sight or even lust at first sight. It was good down-to-earth talking and meeting someone who was interesting, with lovely manners, and handsome to boot!

It was about a week later he invited me to a casual bike ride along the river. I thought, 'That's nice and no heavy commitment in that,' so I said yes. And for me, because I was so jaded with the dating scene, I was always thinking friendship.

We made arrangements to meet at a park with our bikes. So here I am in casual clothes waiting, then suddenly in came this sporty-looking guy in the usual serious bike riding clothes. I have to say I was intimidated! He had just ridden from his house to the park which was about fifteen kilometres away. I was thinking to myself, 'Gee, I had only had my bike for the last month or so and serious riding was not on my radar!' I secretly think he was trying to impress me and he did (nice butt!). That day was lovely, and we enjoyed each other's company. When it was time to say goodbye, I said my farewells, packed my bike away into the back of the car, and left.

Rather quickly!

Looking back, I have come to realise that I was really starting to like him, someone totally different to the type of guy that I had dated in the past. This was all part of my journey, meeting new people, trying something different, and not labelling people or things that came my way. Just accept and trust.

It was about a month later that he invited me to go roller skating. We had talked, and he texted me in between our next get-together and stayed in contact. I said yes to skating as I had done a lot of this in my teenage years. I was so looking forward to reliving my youth all in an afternoon. We had a lot of fun just skating around. The image of this guy uninhibitedly performing the 'dead cockroach' during one of the theme sessions certainly brought those adolescent memories flooding back!

Once the session was over, I suggested we pick up some lunch and take it back to my place. Little did I know my hubby would say that this was me seducing him. Hahahaha! Anyway, we stopped at my favourite pub, ordered lunch, and took it back to my place. We opened up some wine and enjoyed ourselves in each other's company. My darling hubby never ended up leaving my place, and he became 'The One', my soulmate, and our lives together started.

We both knew what we wanted in our lives and future. If we felt it, then we were prepared to give it a go. We both had children from previous marriages, and including them altogether was going to be interesting to say the least and so we did.

We were married two years later, and the day was absolutely wonderful. A beautiful garden setting, cocktail on arrival, dancing into the night . . . but that's another story!

It is now seven years since we met, and we tell each other every day that we love each other. We never leave without this simple but beautiful sentiment. He tells me every single day that I am beautiful, and we always kiss hello and goodbye. We flirt with each other with text messages during the day. These are the little things that we like to do to nurture our relationship.

We also decided between us that the silly games some couples play, for example, silent treatment and expecting the other half to know exactly what we are thinking is not part of our relationship. We choose to speak up and let the other person know how we are feeling and why.

One thing I was never told or taught as a child or teenager was that the idea of dreaming was ok at any age and to trust that the universe only wants the very best for you. All you have to do is ask and so I *did*!

My husband is truly my soulmate and my best friend. We laugh with and at each other all the time. We certainly have our disagreements, but they are always done with respect for who we are as individuals.

And the list? Well, everyone can have their own list, an opportunity to dream that special someone into their life.

> 'It sometimes takes a state of solitude to bring to mind the real power of companionship.'

—Stephen Richards

Marlene Richardt
Email: Marlene@linksforlife.com.au
Website: links4life.com.au

PUBLISHING ON AMAZON

Desire: Publish a Book and Sell It on Amazon
Time Frame: Five Years

In October 2009, I was reading many books, and one in particular really moved me. It was *The Law and the Promise* by Neville Goddard. It was a collection of stories from people who had used their imagination to attract something they really wanted. I loved this book. I was inspired to try and use what Neville talked about to do the same in my life. I always feel that reading quietly is the easiest way for me to improve how I feel. It's the moments of reading people's triumph over a problem and turning it into a solution that still to this day is one of my favourite pastimes.

It really got me thinking. In this book, there were stories of people that attracted trips, won money at the horse races, built a block of apartments with no money, and there was one woman who even attracted so much money she never had to work. She had bought a car, a place to live, and many other things she wanted just by using her imagination while really poor and destitute. She didn't even have enough to buy an outfit for an interview. So I was reading this book night after night. It lifted my spirits high, and I started to apply it. I myself went on to manifest five trips overseas fully paid in six years and a BMW paid cash and I tripled my income, and I moved into a beautiful apartment. I was on a roll, and I thought to myself, 'I so love these stories. Wouldn't it be wonderful to write my own book of inspiring stories and contribute just like Neville Goddard had in the 1960s?'

Neville talks a lot about 'living in the end' meaning living in the end result of the desire that you want. Living 'from' it. For example, you want a new home and have found it, but you don't have the money. So Neville suggests falling asleep in this bed in the current home you live in but mentally fall asleep in the new bed in the new home. Look out that window. What would you see? Living 'from it' and not thinking 'of it' which therefore generates the feeling of satisfaction and peace and joy of having the desire fulfilled.

So I decided to do as he suggested. I applied this to writing my own book. I would visualise holding a book in my hands; it was my book, already written with all the wonderful stories in it. At this stage, I had no idea how I was going to attract enough stories to do it, but I didn't let that deter me. I knew that if I had a desire, then the universe had the power to fulfil it. I saw the words 'you have to believe it to see it' written on the cover. I saw old world French inspector Clusoe on the cover, that kind of style with a magnified glass and irregular fonts. I found out later that Wayne Dyer already had a book with that title, so I had to change the name. I was watching the series 'A Person of Interest' on TV with John and Finch, and I loved it and then pop! There was my new title; it was that simple.

Five years ago, there wasn't a strong Facebook presence like there is now, so I waited to meet people with a good story to be able to write them. I started with my own, sometimes writing only once every couple of months. It was a very slow process. I met Sashi, Kim and Greg in the retail store I was working in at the time. Their stories are in the book. I then did a course in 2012–2013 on the Law of Attraction, and all my fellow students were perfect candidates for the stories that followed.

So although this manifestation took a long time, it was so worth the wait. Interviewing the individuals was exciting, and I feel really blessed that they have shared what they wanted and how they did it with us.

I then was given a book by my friend Lyndall whom I worked with, and she said to me, 'Perhaps you can contact the publisher of this book to see if they will publish your book.' I did and sent them the book on USB. Four months went by, and they had done nothing. I was getting annoyed; they weren't communicating or doing anything. I called and asked the publisher where they were up to, and they told me, 'Oh I think we saw your *USB somewhere*.' I was livid by this stage and told them to forget it and they were fired. That night, I got online, and in ten minutes, I found a new publisher in the USA and I self-published it to retain 100 percent creative control of my work. Xlibris was fantastic from the beginning, and they communicated extremely well and followed through on everything and the experience was effortless. They guided me through every step and were always available if I wanted to ask anything at all. I wasn't going to share this story, but a few people I trust around me told me to include it that it would help another budding storyteller to do the same.

And also, the tortoise wins the race. I have been a hare all my life and can see why now the tortoise does win. Slow, steady small steps weekly have been the lesson here. It doesn't matter how long it takes. It's the fact of moving towards completion. I saw that book in my mind in 2009. I had no idea how I was going to do it. The path lights up as you start, the right people appear, and eventually in 2014, the book was in my hands.

ADORABLE

Desire: A Pony
Time Frame: Three Years

'Isn't it adorable?' nine-year-old Kristelle announced to me and my friends Gail and Rick (her auntie and uncle) when she held up her pink polka dotted bikini. I had to smile because it was, but not as much as she was telling us about it with such delight.

Last week, I decided to ask the universe for the rest of the stories to finish this book. I asked that they came easily from interesting people, and then I let it go and didn't think much more of it.

I went to see Gail and Rick, my dear friends, and Kristelle was dropped off by her older brother to spend the afternoon with them. She came in quite confident, and after a short period, she started to talk about a pony she had. I thought how wonderful that was since most young girls at some point in childhood desire one. Kristelle started to tell me all about it, unasked by me.

At four years old, Kristelle's mum had horses; she trained them and sold them. She started at the age of four thinking about having a pony of her own. She told me she thought about it during the day and also she would regularly dream about it. I asked her if she thought about it before sleep. She corrected me, 'In sleep, in sleep.'

She saw he had brown 'skin' and a cute face, and he was small. She rode him in the dream, and she felt really excited. She had lots and lots of dreams over the three years. She asked her mum to get her one and her mother said she was saving.

I asked Kristelle straight away if she believed that she would get one. She confidently answered 'yes'. There was no doubt. She would pray to Jesus 'Bless me with one' and got stronger and stronger in her belief. She earnestly informed me that the feeling of having it grew over time.

'I thought if I said to Jesus, "I will get one" (pony). My imagination has the power. My brain tells me that. I need one, and it's fun! Jesus and God want you to be happy, so if you keep saying, "I won't get it, then you won't."

'I believe I can be successful. I can show my mum I can do that. I don't believe Jesus can do it all. I think my brain can do most of it. If Jesus can do it, I can do it.'

Before I interviewed Kristelle, I told her I wanted nine more stories for my book. She said, 'Now you need eight.' I hadn't even asked her yet to include her story.

She recounted that when dreaming about the pony, she had thoughts of 'I will get one because I am lucky. Talking to Jesus, I will get it.' She rode ponies at friend's places and also rode ponies in her dreams. The day she got the pony, when she was seven years old, she was *really* excited. When she saw him arrive in the float, she started screaming with excitement. She told me it was the happiest day of her life. She said she had ridden him mentally in her mind so many times that she just knew how.

'I know my imagination works. I did it about five days a week, thinking "of" it, having it. The pony's name was Brownie . . .' Oh, she has three ponies now, two years later!

Kristelle also informed me that she wants to grow up and be successful to help other kids ride ponies. 'I believe in it since I was four. I need it (pony). It's in me because Mum was a horse riding person. Horse riding is a good thing for you because it's healthy. That's what my mum said.'

Kristelle also used her imagination for running races. She was in grade three. She knew she was running the next day against grade fours. She prayed, 'I come first or second.' She prayed that prayer the day before the race and 'in it.' 'In it?' I asked. 'Yes, in it, while running.' She said to herself just before the race, 'If I don't win it's OK. It's not about the winning, it's about the fun.'

She told me of some parents that put too much pressure on kids.

She now dreams of being a surgeon. She says, 'I want to see the inside, what goes wrong. Looking at the inside is fun. I believe I can do it. Everything can be fixed you know, friendships, buildings, and bodies.' Kristelle told me that she watches hospital surgical shows with her brothers who are older, but they leave the room and want to throw up.

I was gobsmacked at this nine-year-old black belt manifestor. I asked what her dad was in all of this. 'He is not around. He's gone.' She then paused, smiled, and earnestly told me, 'I can have a happy life even without a dad.'

I was emotionally moved beyond words today. Who would have thought?

Krisandajames@gmail.com

FOCUS

Desire: Selling Two Blocks of Land
Time Frame: 1. Two Weeks
                 2. Three Months

Two years ago, I subdivided my 2160M2 Principal Place of Residence (PPR) from one block of land to three blocks of land.

My house was located in the middle of the block, so there was one block at the front and one block at the back.

The aim of the subdivision was to sell the front and back blocks and keep the house that I would rent later on.

What was the desire?

> *Selling the two blocks of land*
>
>> → *Time Frame: First block two weeks and the second block three months.*
>
> *Receiving the land titles from the Department of Natural Resources and Mines (the wait is usually two weeks)*
>
>> → *Time Frame: Two Days.*

1. *Selling the two blocks of land*

Time Frame: Two weeks and three months.

The desire was to sell the two blocks although the subdivision wasn't even started.

I put them on the market end of September 2012.

After two months of inactivity from the agent's side, I decided to contact another real estate agent. It was in December 2012. I was told that it was a slow time to sell properties as it was the school holidays, but end of January or beginning of February 2013, the market would increase again.

I was not satisfied by the fact that I had to wait two more months.

My goal was to sell the two blocks of land fast. I wanted to be certain that all the expenses related to the works performed on the subdivision would be quickly refunded.

I knew that using the Law of Attraction will help me realise my objectives rapidly. The universe needed to be aware of what were my desires. I had to let 'Him' know that I strongly wanted to be successful in doing this subdivision.

I started by following the steps below:

> I talked about the sale positively, that is, *The two blocks of land are sold.*
> I repeated it several times a day.
> I put a photo of each block on the fridge door with *sold* written on it.

1. I visualised the blocks with the real estate sign with a big *sold* on it. I stand in the middle of each block seeing this big *sold* sign.
2. I wrote the following in my goals book:

> *I trust and I believe that the blocks of land are sold and that the contract of sale is unconditional.*

And in my gratitude journal, I wrote the following:

I am so happy and grateful that the blocks of land are sold.
Thank you, thank you, and thank you.
Every day, these positive affirmations were read silently or loudly.

Two weeks after starting my Law of Attraction processes, around 3 January 2013, I received a call from the real estate agent who wanted to see me for a meeting. I thought that he wanted to catch up and tell me how many views the advertisement had attracted.

To my surprise, a buyer was in the office ready to sign a contract of sale for the back block that he fell in love with. After agreeing on the price, the contract was signed with a cooling off period of five days.

Wow! The first success! But before celebrating, I waited for the cooling off period to be over.

So the back block was sold. I had to focus now on the front block.

My next-door neighbour was amazed how quick the sale was, but he was convinced that it would take much more time to sell the other block.

Front blocks of land with street frontage are hard to sell. It would surely take six to eight months before I get a 'bite.'

I could show him otherwise.

I followed the same steps I did for the back block and

1.   I believed, believed, believed, and trusted.
2.   I stayed focus on this strong desire to sell the block.
3.   I spent time every day visualising and being grateful.
4.   A big *sold* was written on its photo.

The real estate agent was catching up with me regularly. I didn't lose faith.

Then, in mid-March 2013, a potential buyer showed his interest, and a contract of sale was signed at end of March 2013.

Second success. I was over the moon. Wow, again!

In total, it took me three and a half months to sell two blocks of land using the Law of Attraction.

Trust and believe that everything is possible is the key to success and accomplishment. The universe is there for all of us, and if we persist, our desires are surely provided.

➤   *Receiving the land titles from the Department of Natural Resources and Mines (the wait is usually two weeks)*

Time Frame: Two Days.

The subdivision works started at end of April 2013 until end of June 2013.

As the land was divided into three lots, I had to get three different land titles of the property from the Department of Natural Resources and Mines. This would allow the banks to settle the finances.

So, I had to go through the following steps:

1.   After the completion of the works, I waited for the city council to release the 'as construction plan' which took one month (26th of July),
2.   Then, I sent the 'as Construction Plan' to the solicitor who received it on 29 July.
3.   The solicitor forwarded the plan to the Department of Natural Resources and Mines on 30 July. It usually takes them fifteen days to release the three land titles.

I must explain that on 16 August 2013, I was going overseas, and I started to be concerned about the delay. I counted the days (without the *weekends*), and it was obvious that the titles would be released around 19 August after I was gone. I was out of the country for five weeks and I couldn't make the buyers wait any longer. The settlement had to occur before I left on 16 August.

In my daily meditation, I asked for the titles to be delivered and the settlement to happen before Friday, 16 August.

I prayed and visualised the documents and the finances being released. I drew three land titles and wrote on them 'released before 9th of August'.

Several times a day I said:

I trust and I believe that the three land titles are released now and that the settlement is occurring now through the Divine Power of the universe's own good and riches

I am so happy and grateful that the three land titles are released now and that the settlement is happening before 16 August.

Then I let it go, saying to the universe that I was ready to receive.

On Friday, the second of August, I received an email from my solicitor advising me that he had the three land titles back and that the settlement would occur on Friday, 9 October.

I had to postpone the date to 15 August as one of the buyers was asked by his bank to deliver some more documentation.

The settlement occurred on 15 August, and the money was on my bank account when I left on 16 August.

Once again, the universe had delivered my desires.

I was and still am so grateful.

Claudine Dufroux
www.blossom50andover.com

THE HOUSE AND
THE TENANTS

Desire: 1. Rental House
   2. Tenant for My House

Time Frame: 1. Two Weeks
     2. Two Days

The desire was to find a *rental house closer to the City to live in with my family.*

I lived on an acreage for fourteen years, thirty-five kilometres from the city, and loved it. I knew that the chance to find this kind of rental property close to the CBD was rare, and I had to accept the idea that I would have to live on a small block of land.

I started my search in *mid-December 2013* on RealEstate.com and in the newspapers. I was looking for a three-to-four bedroom house, two bathrooms, spacious living area, an office, a big garage/shed, and a yard for my dog, with a rent that matches my budget.

Every day, I was visiting houses, excited about what I was going to discover. Was it the *day* I would find the ideal rental property? But, at each time, I was coming back from the inspections disappointed by what I had seen. The houses were either too small with an acceptable garden or large but with a tiny yard and garage and far too close to the neighbours.

I was persistent in my search, monitoring the web for new listings. In addition to surfing the web for listings, I told all my friends and acquaintances that I was looking for a place.

I was sure that there was a rental house somewhere around the city that was similar to what I was looking for. It was there in the universe waiting for me to find it.

1. *I started to talk positively about this house I was going to find very soon.* (I wanted to find it before the end of December 2013).
2. *I visualised it on a big block. (I forgot about the small land around the city.)*
3. *I repeated a few times a day, 'The house I am looking for is somewhere and I am finding it now, with the universe's help and guidance. I trust, I believe, and I am ready to receive'.*

The second week of looking, I went to visit the same kind of places. Every morning, I was getting up saying the same affirmations. I put a photo of a random house on a big block of land on the fridge; it helped me visualising it.

Then on the third day of the last week of December 2013 (second week of searching), I read a small ad in regards to a big property to look after. I rang the real estate agent who asked me if I was able to maintain a big block of land. My answer was 'yes, of course'. She was looking for new tenants who could look after this place as if it was their own house.

I visited it. To my amazement, it was an old big house built in the middle of a 4000-m² land, located within fifteen minutes to the city centre. Furthermore, the houses in the neighbouring were all multimillion-dollar houses. I could act *as if* I was a millionaire too.

It had four bedrooms, one bathroom, a large living area, a roomy office, and a . . . *huge* garage/shed. The rent was within my budget.

Wow, once again, the universe rewarded me! The joy for this manifestation was indescribable.

1. The second desire was *to find some tenants for my PPR.*

In the beginning of January 2014, I had some interviews with a few different real estate agents and chose one that suited my needs. I told her that the house would be available on 20 January. I still had some things to fix like the swimming pool fence and plumbing, and I had to comply with the swimming pool fence, water consumption, and smoke alarm.

Once the agent had received all the compliance certificates, she advertised the property the second week of January 2014.

I had no doubt whatsoever that the house would be rented quickly. I trusted and believed that some people would love to live there. I printed a photo of it and wrote on it:

> *'My home is rented as of 20 January 2014 on a long-term basis, and the tenants are very happy there'.*

The day after the ad appeared on the web, around fifteen people showed their interest in the property. An inspection was organised, and one family was chosen.

They moved in on 21 January 2014, and since then are happily enjoying their life in their rental home.

It was a quick manifestation. I never doubt that it would happen quickly. Imagining that people were happy living in the house I have always taken care of made my heart sing. I was happy; therefore, I was in alignment with my desire.

Claudine Dufroux
www.blossom50andover.com

LAW COLLEGE

Desire: Admission into My Favourite College
Time Frame: One Month

It was in 2010. I completed my twelfth grade, and I had to join a college to pursue law. At that point in time, I had no resources as my dad had fallen ill and was not able to provide any sort of financial assistance to me. Well, I couldn't ask him. I was totally helpless. My dad made sure that if I needed any money for the college, I could ask him, but I didn't. I had no idea that the law colleges in the city had started to conduct an entrance exam which was compulsory for a student in order to gain the admission into the colleges. I was too late as the entrance exams were just over in all the colleges, and when I heard this, I slumped emotionally.

After two sleepless nights, I decided that I should start looking for an avenue so that I can pay the fee to my college. The next day, I personally approached several banks to convince them to give me a scholarship to pursue law. Every bank declined. They also made harsh comments on my choice of education (law). I almost broke down on the road trying hard to handle the pressure and the feeling of rejection. The next day, I decided to go to a particular college, fill an application, and pick up the prospectus even though I had no chance of getting into the college because I had not written the exams let alone clearing them. As I left the college, something in me shifted and I caught a bus back home with a change in feeling. I was feeling determined to get into this college no matter what. I decided to ignore all the facts and what other people were telling me. I took the same bus route everyday which would pass in front of my college building just to *feel* that I *had already got my admission.* I used to *feel* grateful. As the bus approached the college building, I felt immense excitement. After a few days of doing the same thing while being grateful for getting into the college despite all the things that were totally opposite, a distant family member was ready to pay the fee through a trust set up by them. But still I had not got the green signal from the management of the college. That day, late afternoon, I got a call from the college management asking if I could come down to the office so that I can have a word. I went the next day. The principal of the college called me into the office, and we spoke. I

73

also mentioned that I love law and stuff like that. I was also sure that there were no seats left in the college as the admission for that year was coming to an end. It was in the end of the conversation that the principal mentioned that she had a 'feeling' after going through my application and hence she called me over. She then said, 'Welcome, Gautham. I have high expectations of you.' I was so freaking excited. I went to the washroom and literally screamed. That day, I paid my fees and enrolled myself for the course.

Here are some things that I did to get that admission in the college.

1. Initially, I came across *The Secret Book*. I read it and reread it.

To make sure I got to the point where I could practice, I also read stories on the secret website.

2. I journaled like a crazy man – Writing all about how happy and grateful I was for making it despite all the hassles on the way. Just feeling the joy and gratitude of having done it, having achieved it.
3. I also listened to Abraham-Hicks. Their videos made me really powerful and repeatedly drilled the fact into my head that I am creating my own reality no matter what.
4. Then came along the journey my favourite teacher Neville Goddard. He is the full package! I wish I had bumped into his teachings a bit earlier because since then I've had many manifestations all reinforcing the fact that I *do create my own reality* every millisecond in my life!
5. A big shout out to Neville for his immortal works, what a wonderful man!
6. Whatever situation you are in and whatever you want to have or be or do literally does not matter when you know this stuff.
7. 'Whatever you desire, believe that you have *received* it and you will.' (Bible quote)

We are all creating our reality 24/7 even if we are not aware of it.

Trust me, you do. Nothing outside of you is doing it for you. No deity external to you is the cause for your life because nothing outside is as powerful as the *being that is within you* nor can anything be.

No Facial Hair

Desire: Perfect Partner
Time Frame: Eighteen Months

My desire was to meet my soulmate, friend, partner with all the qualities I desired, and I wasn't accepting anything less than. I went in as far as how he looked, right down to facial hair. He had to be a family man with children, responsible, and well financially, and I even had what star sign he needed to be, and he had to have a sense of humour.

You know how they say it's what you focus on. I felt strongly about *no* facial hair, even to the point of having resistance to it. So therefore guess what the universe provided? It was everything I desired including the facial hair.

I was with a dating agency. They called me to say, 'We have this guy who is interested in meeting up with you.' So I asked them for all the qualities I desired. Now he ticked all my boxes except that facial hair. So I said, 'OK, no worries. I will still meet him.' After looking at the profiles that they had already sent me, I was very definite and said no. So he called me that day. We are being together ever since that day and are now married as well. The thing was I had a vision board full of pictures and words of what I desired in my relationship. My husband also had a vision board of what he desired in a relationship. We both got more than what we asked for. And yes, he still has facial hair, which in the scheme of things really wasn't that important. It so is what you focus on. Whether it's what you want or what you don't want. It took me approximately twelve to eighteen months to manifest my desire.

I only did a vision board. At that time, I didn't know too much about the Law of Attraction. I did up my vision board of my ideal man after I split up from my boyfriend in March 2005. So learning from that relationship, my first husband, and other guys I went out with, I was very clear on what I wanted this time round. I decided I would take nothing less than what I wanted. On it, I stuck a photo of a man who had a good body and dark hair and photos of couples in love. Then I wrote words like he had to be good looking in my eyes, be family man, and have had children, be responsible. I also wrote that I am attracted to him and he is attracted to me, and we have the same interests and like the same music. He is around the same age of mine (not more than six years), financially independent, and my equal. He has to be open and willing to look at himself and be into self-growth, a spiritual man, confident, gentle, and supportive. I have to feel safe. He loves me for who I am, is trustworthy, and has a sense of humour. He sees my worth and is my friend. It was also very important to me that he wasn't an alcoholic or problem drinker. The vision board was a continuing reminder to me of what I wanted. Along with these, I told the dating agency that his sign should be either water or earth. In my mind though, I was thinking Taurus. I also told them what age he should be. I told them that he definitely had to be a family man and should have dark hair. I just kept looking at my vision board. And every time I'd get a call from the agency, I kept telling them time and again what I was looking for. What was very important though and I know helped me heaps was I went in with no attachments. It actually looked like I was going to have fun, meet new people, and make friends, and if I found my soulmate, that was a bonus. It took me about fourteen months. We spoke on the phone for the first time in May 2006. We hit it off on our first phone call. It wasn't until I first met him the very next day that I knew I was attracted to him. I loved his eyes and his smile. My husband's name is Ian. Ian and I don't mind if you use our names.

Leith Jeffrey
Facebook page: 2 Beextraordinary
Tapping Into the Power Within.

HOW I GOT MY
ASS TO EGYPT

Desire: A Trip Somewhere Hot
Time Frame: Two Weeks

When I was a newbie of the Law of Attraction, I read and reread *The Secret* by Rhonda Byrne, and second time, it hit me. I started saying to everybody I was going on holiday. At this time, I was reading *The Magic* for the first time and applying gratitude in my life like crazy. Man, my friends were ready to call the nut house and take me in! But I was in a happy place and enjoying life to the max (still do; no, I am lying. I am enjoying it even more *now*, lol!). So a week before I was on the plane, I went into meditation (visualisation) and saw myself, and was feeling the plane take off. You know when the nose is up, we are all hanging almost upside down, and I could feel even the turbulence, telling another person, think of it as an attraction. I had a smile on my face and was laughing out loud in my meditation state, because it was funny. Haha! I then, in meditation state, got myself into first class. I made up a story that it was overbooked and if I mind to sit in first class. Well, that was seriously really comfortable. The feeling of a big chair, feet up straight, and champagne, mmmm, I loved it! I could even almost taste the champagne. Mmmm!

Well, still (two weeks before manifestation) in the same week, I told my friends about my trip to Egypt, and one of my girlfriends asked me, 'How much should it cost?' I was like, 'Uhhmm, no matter the price, I just want swimming pool, lots of service at the pool and palm trees around me, and most important, *the sun* on my face, just relax, completely nothing else.' After a while, I had not spoken to my friends and I was like, 'Hey, my daughter is going soon to her dad for the first time in my life, since she was born. I have a whole week for myself, so hello, Lord, where is my money or ticket at?' So after a few days, I got an epiphany and that was like joh chick, joh Jackie, how you going on holiday without clothes? I rushed to the guestroom and got out my suitcase. Then I thought to myself, 'What do I need? Well, it's warm where you are going, so . . . OK dresses, dresses, dresses, and so on.' Seven dresses one for each day, and later on, just seven extra. I am a lady. Well, shoes were easy this time because I was off to relax . . . but I thought, 'You never know what will happen because you be chilling during the day, but how about the night life?' OK, got out my bigger suitcase and just threw in a couple of shoes (boom!), underwear, and bathroom stuff and done.

On Tuesday, I asked the Lord, 'Hello, it's almost Friday. What's going on?' Remember, while asking this question, I was still in my crazy ass jolly mood. By asking this and stating it, it doesn't mean that I was desperate. I did this in a fun way.

So I got another epiphany and that was of course to me, 'cause I was like, 'Jacks, you're going abroad, so you best get your passport in there as well . . . check.' OK, my bag was ready. Friends came over asking me why my suitcase was packed. I said, 'I am going on holiday.'

'Where to?'

'Well, where it is warm.'

They were like, 'Oh, well that's Jacks on her ass.'

Wednesday, I went to visit my parents for a lovely chill day evening, and at night, we were gazing at the stars, enjoying each other's company, and boom . . . then the manifestation started to evolve . . . OMG! Hold your horses! Well, you can never get Jackie quiet, not even with meditation, but this time, she was still and crying for an hour long of the joy and love she just received.

So my parents and I were chilling. My darling daughter Jena was sleeping soundly. My mom said, 'Well, this year, we want to go crazy.' (Oh, oh, I was like damzz they be going Jackie style! Haha!) So they said, 'We wanna go crazy this year. Just do not want to check the balance for once.' I was like, 'Yeah, cool, live, yeah yeah, *me pro live*! Haha.' So my stepdad started, 'Well, we want you to help us decide, because we want to help you for the incredible work you have done with Jena (my daughter) and you have done a great job, all by yourself and you deserve a break.' Can you imagine how my head and body was listening? I was like, 'Oh no, what the crap is happening here? Breathe, Jackie.' That's what was going on in my mind. 'Breathe, woman, breathe. Hear the man out. Pfff!' So he continued, 'But, (the 'but' did not shake my beliefs at all. I was like, 'Oh well, I am still listening.') I would also love to help your cousin out, from Uganda, to come to Holland and get a sense of how things work here, 'cause it's good for her education and all that.' Well, you can guess my answer. 'Oh yes, please bring her and give her an opportunity for three months here.' They looked shocked like crazy, and I just said, 'I know my spring break is on its way. I will get my rest and sun and palm trees.' So we sat for a while. I missed them for about half an hour. Then they came back outside, and drum roll please, drum roll please, wuahahah . . . hold on to you, whatever you have near you know . . . My stepdad said, 'Well, I and your mum talked, and we are so proud of you, being so unselfish, that you let someone else enjoy rather than yourself (little did they know that I was already aligned with my suitcase and palm trees in my vision of my own truth), and before that and because we really want to do something for you and your cousin, you can go on holiday. The (in shock now, while he speaks, or coma, or just the sound of a flat line) cost is not important, and your cousin can come as well.' Shock, shock, shock! OK, got out of shock and just started crying like a baby. Damzz, I never knew I had so many tears to shed. I almost had my own swimming pool right there and then lol!

After almost an hour of only gratitude and tears, they asked, 'Well, what's your answer?' Uh uhm uhm uhm tears rolling, yessss, while being hugged, because I think they never saw me cry like that damzz . . . Parents in shock, Jackie in shock, so thank God, miss little J was sound asleep!

So next day, Thursday, I woke up as if it was a dream. I was like, 'No, Jackie, you were not that hammered, and if you were, those tears you drop, they got you sober. Haha.' So I woke up and waited and waited, and my stepdad came to me and said, 'Hello, are we going to book the trip?' Almost saw my life flash right in front of my eyes. Damzz, you can imagine that gratitude I had as a single mum, raising a kid alone and hardly no help from the dad, so it was me and her 24/7, so its excitement and you read joy and gratitude. I was amazed that I got a break. Wohhh.

On Friday, off I was to the airport, by train, and people were like, never seen a person who grins so much! Hahaha! I reached the airport early and got my suitcase checked in, while greeting everyone there with a smile and sometime with a grin and sometimes, I could control myself, I gave a smile, while looking for the smoking room. Oh, yeah, I found a smoking room called Jameson. So bag checked in, a Jameson, and a cigi. Wuahahhah, I was in heaven! I was truly a little kid in Disneyland, wow!

It was boarding time. I didn't get into business class, *but* they had so much room that I had three chairs for myself. Now, how is that for first-class service, feet up, and with the book *The Magic* on my lap! I was off.

When I started visualising all these, I had 150 euros as savings and got a free ticket and pocket money and over there treated like a queen. Wauw! Wauw! I had all included breakfast and dinner, and most of the people didn't get that, this all started on the evening of my arrival. I got my first free dinner, from a local person there, and then a free camel ride and then a free bookmark, with my name written on it in Arabic. I think you can imagine the rest of my awesome holiday. Oh, just a little one to encourage to stay focused and positive. The Lord sometimes was testing me. At the end of the holiday, I had to pay, and guess what, my bank account said no balance. Say what? Second time, I went all the way to click the amount I needed. Boom, thing just throws out my card! At this time, I was thinking, 'I am ready for Holland. It has been fun. Now, give me the money . . . please.' The third time, again with no balance, so you do understand, I could have gone mad that the next time I try, the card will not come back. I said, 'I am the force of Love. I am the force of Joy, and this is gonna go well.' Well, the fourth time got it in, and Hallelujah! Amen! Praise all Gods!

Love/Gratitude, the Law of Attraction being clear and the most important *have faith*. Hope you enjoy, and remember, there is always magic ready to happen *for you*. Just let it happen . . . May the force of love, peace, and understanding always be with you.

www.facebook.com/jackie.dewit

Cool Side of Jackie

Desire: Soulmate
Time Frame: Two Weeks

After my marriage with my first true love, that passed in 2010, may he rest in peace, I lost thirty kilogram effortlessly, but that manifestation story is for another day, or actually briefly it's easy, 'live in the end' (by Neville Goddard). Neville says to live in the end result in your imagination, and it will come. Since then I have been single for about seven years with on and off relationships. I started most of them knowing it was OK and reading manifestation stories and not understanding what I was doing wrong. However, I also did not really care. I could manifest holidays, things, money but a relationship with a man was whole different ball game.

Then I started asking myself a lot of questions why was my soulmate not appearing? (When people asked me why I was still single, I used to make jokes saying it was because my prince was on a snail instead of a horse.) And what was it that I was looking for in a soulmate? Especially the last question I was asking, what do I want? I was never really clear on that. So I kept getting the unclear relationships, and do not get me wrong, I knew I was doing it 'cause every time I would start to visualise a man, I could not see the complete picture or feel it intensely, so guess what? That's what I received.

Last year, I was like OK I am now ready to meet him, and I have no commitment issues anymore. (I was stating and making this assumption real.) I am ready. I want to meet my man tonight. But before this evening, I had seen us together getting married and saying our vows. That was when I knew, it was going to happen, 'cause I had so much love that day 'our wedding day.' So I went out with the strong will that it was done. I did meet Mr Right, not my soulmate, but Mr Right for that particular time. I had been singing a song for a very long time and feeling it as real as I could 'We found love in a hopeless place,' and that was true. I did find love, and it was a hopeless place. It's a place where you go when everything else is closed and your body still has a lot of energy. It was also love at first sight, and that is something I have 'wondered' for a long time as well. I want to know what love at first sight is, crazy ass me. And a friend had just asked me,

'What is your type?' And thinking back now, it was not me who was ready, but my friends always asked me, 'What is your type, because you are always alone?' And at that moment, I pointed at a guy near me. Be careful of what you wish for! The Law of Attraction at its best!

Well, after a few months, nope, that was not him! Shocked, but I knew I had to let him go. I continued to be my own happy self again. And before I started this, I revised the situation in my imagination, how I wanted it to be (technique by Neville Goddard). All other relationships felt good with the old Jackie, but not with the new. And I don't know what happened, and all of a sudden, I decided to have a good talk with myself. I wanted my soulmate. I wanted a man who is kind, caring, and as strong as I am. And I thought really hard. 'Jackie, what is it that you would love in a man?' I have been asking myself for a while now, but I never gave myself the chance to answer the question. And this time I was ready, no backing down, full of self-love, and let's get this future into the present. So I started to see myself as I would love to see myself when I am with my soulmate, imagining us going out to the opera and me wearing an awesome evening dress (red of course) and we going out to celebrate our thirtieth anniversary of marriage. Felt so real, and I let it go. I did not contradict it at all. I had been thinking of how awesome it would feel to be loved by a man, and what it would feel like, so I just used my ex-husband in heaven to get some of the extra feeling, and after a while, I just did things easy. Like when I went to bed, I would kiss him goodnight and say, 'I love you' (kissing air), and when I would find myself not believing me, when I went to bed, I would say, 'Oh, soon my darling would be back from his business trip.' I would even sometimes go further as to say which country he was and how proud I am of him being there and supporting the family. 'Oh, I can't wait to see him again and hold him in my arms.' I had a lot of these moments that I would just let it play itself out. Another time, I would get a place mat extra and set the table as if he was there with me and Jena, my daughter. She would ask, 'For who is that?' I would say, 'For my prince.' She is a kid, and she knows how to play imaginary, so she did not mind. P. S. I almost forgot to say what got me into imagination. Remember I told you I did not know what I wanted in a man? Well, I knew now, because I listened to the answer of the question I asked. And that was I want a Jackie in a male form, and I specified in saying, the new Jackie, because the old was less wise and was not aligned with what life had in stored for her. Because I was so in love with me, and I thought, 'Hey, another Jackie, the cool side of Jackie would be so awesome and amazing!'

But before I met him and started to visualise, I also asked God to give me a few signs that were aligned, because I was done with the old me and I was ready to commit for the very last time, till death do us part. So I asked that one of the hints would be that Jena my daughter and he would have the best click ever the first time they met. And as I asked, so it was. I could not believe it. I was still sceptic. Well, let's continue why it was him.

We forget, sometimes, how much feeling we have given in the past in a certain situation or imagination, but it is all still in the vortex of creation. I had always wanted to be a single mum and boom! Funny thing was I had forgotten all about that, but it was something I had had in mind since I can remember, but I forgot, and guess who reminded me after the divorce? My mother-in-law. 'Oh, Jackie, you always wanted to be a single mum, right?' I was shocked to hear this from her.

OK, OK, OK, I know, this all has to do with my soulmate. Stay with me.

I have had a lot of dreams in life that have come true (fortune-teller predictions). So I had a dream of my soulmate, pure love, and all from the age of sixteen and seventeen years old always came back once in a while. I never understood it. I could not put into pieces, and every time, it was always the same ending. He had to go, and we will be soon together. I just need to arrange things. So a few years back learning about the art of revision, by Neville Goddard, (changing your past), I decided I am going to change this. This is so pure, this love, and why can't I be with him every time? I was like I know the law of life. You create whatever you want! I was going to change this, but I could not. Then I tried to see his face and could not see it. I tried to make his hair black, and I could hold the hair colour for about five seconds and boom, gone again. So I let that crazy ass dream go, not knowing it was about to happen in real life.

OK, now almost to the part where we met. I had a girlfriend that had a boyfriend and was seeing someone else on the side. I really wanted to eat her head off, but every time, I was forced with my friend to say, 'there is no good or bad' and I had to constantly remind myself and I was pissed off, damn, because it was not once but twice that she had had 'an affair.' So I was like OK, this has so much to do with me, but still not knowing how. But after I accepted her and her way of life, it all became clear, my dream came clear, and so many years later, bam in my face.

Remember I told you I could not see his face, my soulmate, in my dreams? Well, the night we met, I was for once not drunk. Little did it help me, hahaha! So we had a click that evening when I met him. He wanted a kiss and a hug, and I was like OK, OK, and the people that know me, I would resist like crazy. But OK, he went on his merry way, and I went mine. And guess what, I had no clue what he looked like, completely no idea. I remember everything about that night, people we saw and met, but him, for some reason, I couldn't remember. Two weeks later, we hooked up again, and I was resisting, but still drawn to hook up. So we did. I opened the door. Man, I thought damn, Richard Gear is in the house! Sean Connery the younger years is in the house! Oh, ja, please! I was dating younger men for the last couple of years, and last year for the first time an older one than me, shocker! And also this I had to accept to meet my soulmate. I remember also getting hints as in how old he was. I have something with car license plates, and the last time I almost had a heart attack reading the birth year. I remember saying, 'What? Much older than the last? Oh, no, cannot be true!' Oh, ja! Another thing was also the number three. I had made that my lucky number involving relationships, as in, one female, two male, and three a child, so I made that my number of a family. And of course, his company car had Mr Three and his own car as well! It was creepy!

So back to the first both side sober evening date. Oh my, I had to keep my Jackie cool act on, 'cause I was blown away and nothing he said or did could bring me back to that night to remember him. We laughed. He was like frickin' zen too. I was shocked. Because I am a person, no matter where you put me, I can have a good time with anyone, but for me to be impressed, that is sooo fricking new. So we had an awesome night and lovely conversation. Till that moment, I didn't understand why I was supposed to be OK with my girlfriend's situation. Well, this was a Neville situation. He knew I was going to be his wife, although there was someone else in his life, and I was so shocked that I broke off the contact. I was not even mad at him, but just shocked. I let him be, but mister did not give up, so we continued on a friendship base, 'cause although I knew nothing was good or bad, it is still what for you feels good or bad. So we stayed friends till he made up his mind and we have been happily ever after since.

And of course, you do understand I had to continue to stay in the vortex; after we found each other completely a month later, I decided it was time to hear those lovely three words. I used the whisper technique and voila, and the funny thing was, he had wrote it in an application and I had to show him that he had wrote 'I love you'. Wow, my head kept on spinning! I would love that and that to be done in my house, boom, done! I was still spinning but enjoying the quick manifestation. I told him I was going to go on holiday (that's a manifestation on its own.). I was so aligned with him and could simply whisper anything and also things that I had wanted before meeting him: that I could go on holiday, come back, and my whole house is fixed. Well, holiday happened and so did my makeover bam. That is like a manifestation request for a year now. Wow, this is what I would like to say, just because it has not happened, no matter what it is, it still is in the vortex and you can access it when *you* are ready.

And I thought a soulmate was like a big thing. Oh no, it is the best a person has ever known! Truly, I have always believed in that unconditional and understanding that you see in the movies, but never really captured it as mine. Also as a life coach, he finishes my sentences. When I tell him about a client his like oh this and that and till this day I am still in awe and filled with love each day. This all took only two weeks to manifest from the moment I decided, I wanted my soulmate.

And after a while, I let my guard down and started to get bored. Well, that's when you must activate your powers of manifestation again. And I did, I was like OK, and we went deep into the mainframe on the love part. Now, let's do that with money. What's holding you back in receiving a big pallet of money? Lots of money,

I could always get money no problem at all, but I wanted that big bang theory. Have to have a lot of fun along the way.

I sure hope this will inspire you to believe and let go, and mostly do not contradict it. That's what keeps it away. And remember to be true to yourself, dare to be bold, and ask the right questions.

www.facebook.com/jackie.dewit

THANKS A MILLION

Desire: Millions
Time Frame: Two Months

I never had a problem manifesting money. But a big pile of money, that was a different case. It all goes with your true belief about money. That is what keeps money away. I love money. I love rich people, but I had always a thing like humble. Being too humble about money was keeping me away from money.

I first listened to 'The Science of Getting Rich' by Wallace Wattles on YouTube and noticed I was the one holding me back, as per usual. It was about what I truly believed, and after listening, I still had that feeling of doing good for others with money. And I listened again, and they said, 'Is the service you give others worth the pay?' I was, 'Yes! Yes!' And more questions came, and I kept on answering with yes! 'So why should you not ask for a good pay, if your service is great?' And that hit home! Big time! Because believe me, volunteer work is great (while raising my baby girl). Giving my services for free is wonderful and all, but where is my big bang theory?

I continued listening and being active and efficient as they told me, in my daily routine. OK, OK, then I came across the meditation money flow 'shreem brezee'. I did it once and felt awesome. I am not a meditating type; I am an action figure, but this spoke to me and I loved it! After a few days, I had 100 euros and then 200 euros a week later, from unexpected areas. I was jumping with joy! Money kept on flowing, and then I continued searching everything that had to do with money. I came across 'Conversations with God' (by Neale Donald Walsh). I had seen the movie but not the audio about life's lessons. So I started listening to that and came across the words. 'What you have more of, you can give,' and I thought, 'Damn, I got a lot of love. I give that in return for cash instead of giving a beggar my last money and not feeling good about it,' so the trick here also is, when you give, give it from your heart, and then it will expand. I did this a year ago, had only 20 euros for a whole week, and I was like, 'This is not enough, so better put it to good use.' I bought roses and gave them to strangers on the streets, and boom, before the week was over, I had manifested 150 euros, just like magic. The Law of Attraction at its best!

Back to the millions, I started getting money in the mail. I was for the first time in my life I was in tuned with lots of money! And with a big smile on my face, I was singing, 'I love money and money loves me!'

Then I started an application phone conversation with my best friend and 'living in the end' Neville Goddard style: seeing what we would do with all the money, sending each other pictures, writing our future conversations, and making as real as possible for us. Each day, we would gather pictures of a lot of money and say, 'It's ours. We have it all. We are the source of wealth.' So affirmation and living in the end! Doing this, she would give me Five million euros and ask what I would do with it. I even had a housekeeper, a gardener, a driver, and a pool man. Doing it together helps a lot.

I also listened to Abraham-Hicks often; I got into the vortex on Facebook. And after starting the millionaires club with my girl, we hosted VIP party to really get in to the flow. A friend made a millionaire page, and the links kept on coming. I was guided towards the money. Freely!

Walking one day on the street, I suddenly came across the people from the lottery and they were giving free four-leaf clover plants out to everyone. I felt this was my sign. After a few days, I gave it soil and water, and while knowing my husband and I had one plant, we all of a sudden had two plants. We were shocked, and I knew I was aligned, because it magically multiplied itself. I was happy and shocked.

Seventeen million is the amount I asked for, but I wasn't clear about how I really wanted to spend it, knowing what the amount means, having so much money power and freedom. I won one million and change. I was receiving money in other areas before the big bang win. So once I got clear on how I wanted to spend it and how much everything would be, that's when this amount came. Bam! You have to be really clear and leave it alone. As in, don't doubt. Only keep on giving thanks when doubts pop into your head.

Then after a lot of doubts out of my head, 'cause I always have a small voice telling me you did not win, well, this time that voice came again and I did not win.

But the second lottery I bought, I was like, 'This is it. I am going to repeat the numbers.' I even found out what happens when you win millions, like who you talk to and how you get invited, so played all this out in my head and boom! Unfrickin' believable. Still to this day, I am wondering how. Your mind has a lot of hidden doors to why things do not happen when you want them to happen.

Happy, happy manifesting!

www.facebook.com/jackie.dewit

NOT GIVING MY UTERUS TO THE MEDICOS

Desire: To Not Have an Operation
Time Frame: Eight Months

The year is 1985, and I was thirty-seven years old. I started working as a cashier in a fruit and vegetable market in Mosman, Sydney, NSW Australia. I worked there for six years and was very happy since it was right across the road from where I lived and I could walk to work and I loved my favourite customers. I worked standing up, and the floor was concrete.

My menstruations became really, really heavy and painful, and I knew I had to do something. I prayed every day for guidance and direction and trusted I would get it. I prayed for a solution. I set my intention for this daily and didn't concern myself as to where the help would come from.

One day, it came in the form of a little old lady that came through my till, and she showed me the way. In the meantime, I went to a woman doctor who told me if I didn't have a hysterectomy, it would get worse; she also gave me a letter for a surgeon at the hospital.

I was determined not to give my uterus to the medicos, not at thirty-seven years old, not ever actually! It was mine to keep for as long as I could. So I put that letter in the bin, and after talking to the little old lady that came through my till that day, I decided to follow her advice and go to Chris Cole who was a beautiful, compassionate, loving psychic healer.

I saw Chris Cole three times, and after that time, my menstruations dwindled down to a normal cycle over a month or so. It took eight months to find the answer and then only a month for the recovery.

Today, at the age of sixty-six, I still have my uterus and my menopause was a breeze except for a few hot flushes and no medication at all.

Since then I have sent friends and family members to Chris and they too have experienced great results for all sorts of health issues. One of them being my daughter who went for her tumour (story is in her first book *A Person of Interest*) and she forgot to mention it, so I am mentioning it now because it played a great part in healing that condition at that time.

All these years later, a big thank you to the little old lady angel that came through my till to give me information I really needed, and most of all, big thank you to Chris Cole for helping me save my female bits.

Angela Vivarelli
Agnes's mum
Queenzoomba@gmail.com

THE UNIVERSE BRINGING TOGETHER YEARS OF DREAM BOARD PICTURES INTO ONE PERFECT NIGHT

Desire: Various
Time Frame: Various

I first heard about dream boards when I was nineteen years old. I loved the idea and immediately set about creating one. I went out and bought a bunch of magazines, cut out pictures of mansions, luxury cars, beautiful women, cash, and designer clothes, and pasted them on this big poster board I'd purchased. I slapped the board up on my wall and eagerly began waiting for the good life to arrive. Three months turned into six months, which turned into a year, and I hadn't had a single thing on my dream board manifest in my life. One day, in total disgust, I yanked it down and thought, 'I got conned.'

When I was twenty-one, my business partner and I stopped by his mom's house in Los Angeles. She showed us some kittens that she was looking for people to adopt. After playing with the kittens, I said, 'I think I'll adopt the black one.' My business partner turned to me with a shocked look on his face and said, 'You hate cats! Why would you want to adopt one?' I replied, 'I've never liked cats. But for some reason, I really like this little black kitten.' I took him home, named him Tuffy, and he grew up to be a big black alley cat.

One day, I noticed he was looking particularly dirty. I grabbed him up and decided it was time to give him a bath. I took him into the garage and started washing him. When I was done, I started lifting him out of the sink. Half way out, I almost dropped him in shock. I couldn't believe it. That look!

90

When I had been in college, I bought a poster of a black cat with a hilarious look on its face, as it was being pulled out of a bath, by a nurse. I'd laughed and laughed. I laughed every time I saw that poster I'd put up on my college bedroom wall. I'd loved that poster. Tuffy, all wet, looked exactly like the cat from that poster! I quickly dried him off, let him go, and then sat down to think.

I thought about my dream board experience when I was nineteen and about my college bedroom poster of the wet cat. If it hadn't been for my dream board, I would have thought that Tuffy, looking like the wet cat in the poster, was just a coincidence. However, since I knew about dream boards, I suspected something else was going on. What I couldn't understand was why a wet black cat appeared in my life and not the luxury cars, mansions, and beautiful women. After thinking about it, I realised the difference was emotional. When I'd looked at the cat poster on my wall, it always brought forth positive emotions from me. When I used to look at the dream board, with all the mansions and stuff, they were just pictures. They didn't really mean anything to me. I decided to give dream boards a second chance.

On this second round, I only put up pictures that brought forth a positive emotional response from me. That made all the difference in the world; I began to experience the exciting results I'd always heard possible with dream boards. The following success story is an example of the kind of results I'm experiencing, now that I only post pictures on my dream boards that elicit a positive emotional response when I look at them.

In 2005, I moved to Las Vegas, Nevada. I lived in apartments across the street from the Palms Casino. After working all day, I'd get home at 8 or 9 p.m. On Thursday, Friday, and Saturday nights, I would always hear music thumping as I walked to my apartment. It was coming from the club at the top of the Palms Casino. That always bugged me because I would have liked to be clubbing too, but instead, I was headed inside to start working again. I always spent my evenings and weekends working on my dreams. It was a challenging schedule to keep for a few months. I went on living it for years.

One Friday night, in 2011, I arrived home from my day job, got out of my car, and, of course, heard the music thumping. I stopped and thought, 'One day, I'm going to be staying at a penthouse suite in that casino, instead of being down here with my nose to the grindstone.' I went inside, ate dinner, then sat down to work, and paused a moment. I quickly googled some pictures of the penthouse suites at the Palms. One had an incredible view, overlooking the strip. It was perfect; I could just see myself relaxing in that suite. I printed it out and put it up on my dream board.

In October 2013, a woman named Boom-Boom, who had been living in Korea, moved to Las Vegas. When she was still in Korea, a mutual friend of ours had introduced us via Face book. We were both cautious. But a connection happened. Soon we began dating. Neither of us gambled, although we both enjoyed the strip. So we spent time visiting the different casinos. One day, we decided to stay in one. When Boom-Boom asked me where I'd like to stay, I instantly thought of the Palms Casino because of the picture on my dream board. I mentioned it and then immediately regretted it. I'd always thought, for my first stay, at least, I'd live my dream, in a penthouse suite. I didn't want to spend that kind of money now. I was saving up to open a business in 2014.

We discussed options. The Palms was the only casino I really wanted to stay in. So we went online and looked at rooms. Boom-Boom loves beautiful environments. We found a room that suited her tastes. Although it wasn't a penthouse suite, I had to admit that it was still amazing.

We arrived around 5.30 p.m., on 2 December 2013. The room was just as beautiful as it had been in the pictures. We had a great evening. Around 10 p.m., we fell asleep, only to wake up, shortly after, because the room was suddenly really cold. We couldn't figure out how to fix the room temperature, so we called downstairs. They sent some repairmen up. They couldn't figure out how to fix it either. The front desk told us to pack our stuff. They were moving us to a different room.

We'd been staying on the seventh floor. When we got in the elevator, we realised our new room was on the thirty-fifth floor. After stepping off the elevator, we walked down the hallway.

Boom-Boom wondered that there were so few doors, not the usual room after room. There were only a handful of doors on the entire thirty-fifth floor. We arrived at the door of our new room. As you've probably guessed by now, our new room was a penthouse suite, not only that, but one of the nicest penthouse suites in the entire casino!

We set our stuff down in the living room and began wandering around. The suite had everything: a Bose sound system, a bar with beautiful red and gold tile work, a fire place in front of the bed, matching bathrobes, a Jacuzzi bathtub, and probably the coolest thing was the shower. This was not just a shower but (a shower room) where you turn on the shower and water comes at you from all sides. While that was all great, my favourite thing was the view from the gigantic picture windows. Just like in the picture on my dream board, I could see the side of the original Palms' tower, a stunning view of the strip, and the Rio Casino. The beautiful penthouse suite, with its amazing view, is a classic example of co-creation at its finest.

Boom-Boom's love of beautiful environments combined with my desire to stay in a penthouse suite caused this experience to manifest.

But the story isn't over yet. It gets even better! As soon as I got home from dropping Boom-Boom off at her place, I immediately went to look at my dream board. The first thing I saw was the picture of the penthouse suite at the Palms, with the stunning view of the strip and the Rio Casino (almost virtually the same view we'd had from our penthouse suite). After looking at it, I began looking around at the other pictures on my board. My dream board is gigantic, about four feet wide and six feet tall, the size of a double door. So there are a lot of pictures on it. Suddenly, my eyes stopped. I looked closer. Wow!

In 2008, I'd seen the movie *21*. It was about a team of college students that came to Vegas to count cards. I liked the movie a lot. I especially related to the main character Ben (played by Jim Sturgess). Ben put everything on the line to go after his dream, came to Vegas, and made it happen; plus, he got the girl of his dreams, named Jill (played by Kate Bosworth). There is a scene in the movie where Jill invites Ben up to her penthouse suite overlooking the strip. As I watched that scene, I thought to myself, 'One day that's going to be me.' A few days after seeing the movie, I found a picture online that represented everything I wanted to experience from that movie. I added it to my dream aboard.

Staring at the picture on my dream board, from the *21* movie, I began grinning ear-to-ear for the second time in twenty-four hours. Then, I laughed out loud! *Dream boards are so amazing!* Not only had I gotten to experience the scene in the movie where Jill invites Ben up to her penthouse suite, I'd also gotten the girl! Not only was Boom-Boom super smart like Kate Bosworth's character Jill is in the movie, but Boom-Boom even looked like Kate Bosworth's character Jill does in the movie: down to her brown hair, the classy way she dresses, and even her bob hair cut! Crazier yet! The picture from the movie on my dream board has Ben dressed a bit sloppily compared to Jill, and Boom-Boom had given me a hard time about arriving at a nice casino dressed less nicely than I should be. Amazing!

In closing, I'd like to add a note of thanks to the staff at the Palms. Upgrading our regular room to one of the most expensive suites in the casino was world-class service. I no longer live in Las Vegas. But whenever I return, I know where I'll be staying, always. Thank you.

Author's Bio

Namaste Faustino first learned about the Law of Attraction at the age of eight years. His father had enrolled him in a self-development program for kids, created by the Rosicrucian educational organization. A few months after learning about the Law of Attraction, he successfully manifested a red boom-box radio and his life was never the same. As the years passed, he manifested cash, girlfriends, trips . . . even a millionaire mentor.

In 2014, he took everything he'd learned from manifesting his desires for twenty-nine years and created a Manifesting Checklist. It's easy to use: You start at the top and work down it, item by item. By the time you've reached the bottom, you know you've done everything you need to do to get your desire to manifest.

If you'd like to get the checklist, go to his website: www.mrnamaste.com

THE VERDICT IS 'NOT GUILTY'

Desire: Healthy Body and No Jail
Time Frame: Two Years

On 20 November 2012, Nancy Hunter had a paragliding accident in the Himalayas in Nepal. She had had a great flight that morning and had decided to go on a second one that afternoon despite that she was feeling a bit unwell. She saw the eagles and the vultures dancing in the air, and she wanted to fly to show she could do it. Unfortunately, she didn't listen to her intuition that afternoon, which was saying not to go. Only one out of forty gliders was a woman. Nancy wanted to break through her fear for flying.

That day, while flying she could see everything. The sun was beaming. It was exhilarating! As she turned the glider, she felt a hit mid-turn. She aimed her weight towards the mountains. She felt a hit again. She looked up and saw one wing had collapsed. People were yelling to her to get out of the harness. 'My kids' was her first thought that moment, but oddly, she wasn't thinking of dying.

She hit the ground hard. She had fractured her ribs, and her foot was smashed amongst other things. Eight men rushed to her aid and got a blanket and some bamboo to make splints. One guy had liquid morphine, and he gave her some, but they knew they couldn't let her sleep. It took one and a half hours to carry her down the mountain. From there, they had a four-wheel drive for transport. They made a bed for her and drove her to the nearest hospital one and a half hours away. Bones were sticking out of her ankle through her sock; heel and joint were badly fractured. They had to cut her boot off. Her sock was inside the bones. They wrapped it up and put her in an ambulance for a seven-hour ride through a potholed road to Kathmandu to take her to a better hospital. She was operated on there and remained there for twelve days. She then returned to her home in London, UK.

Nancy's family was in Sydney, Australia. She was enormously helped by friends, but eventually, people had to go back to their lives, and having no family except her two young twin boys, she was torn as to what to do. Nancy had insurance, but she was told they wouldn't pay her if she went to Australia to be cared for by her family.

She was in emotional turmoil and decided she really needed her family, and as soon as injuries were reasonable to fly, she left with her kids to Sydney. She needed them. She needed help to recover and heal and help taking care of the twins. She had argued with the Insurance Company about their decision before leaving the UK.

Her foot had been badly operated on in Nepal. It was crooked. She was re-operated on in Australia. They put plates in her foot. She was told she wouldn't walk again. She stayed five months in Sydney and went to the beach on crutches to swim and recover with the support of family.

She also did acupuncture. She was screaming while doing it. She said, 'It was like the trauma of the injury was being released during these sessions.' The acupuncturist kept repeating to her, 'You will walk again,' and Nancy chose to believe it.

The sand, beach, and ocean were great influencers on the healing of Nancy's body.

Nancy's sister was getting married at that time. Nancy made it to the wedding on crutches which was a milestone in the healing journey. She kept saying to herself, 'I can heal myself,' over and over and over again.

Then she went back to London, UK. She attracted help again. A cranial osteopath treated her for free. She had plates in her foot from the operation in Australia. She had had four operations in total, and she was debating taking the plates out. Six specialists didn't want to take them out. They didn't feel the foot would hold together on its own considering the nature of the accident. Nancy was determined to fully heal herself, and she decided the plates had to come out. She finally found a specialist who would remove them.

Three months later, the bones in her foot healed themselves nicely. Nancy continued believing and said, 'I can heal myself,' despite what six specialists had said.

While Nancy was dealing with all the physical challenges of healing, another storm was heading her way. Her neighbours had reported to council that she had left the country, and when she got back to London, there was a letter under her door to say, 'We have reason to believe you have not been living in your home.' She had been receiving a benefit from the government and a condition of receiving it was that you couldn't leave the country. She was summoned for an interview, and she honestly told them that she had been depressed and her body smashed from the operations and needed the support of family to care for herself and her boys. She spent from May 2013 to September 2013 getting hospital paperwork for them from Nepal (since all records were not on computer there). According to the government, she had broken the law and jail time was a possibility.

It took from October 2013 to May 2014 for them to do the paperwork for Nancy to face court. Jail was looming in the air that whole time which was really difficult to say the least while Nancy was trying to heal her body. At this stage, she was still on two crutches. I met Nancy while doing a global Law of Attraction course online. We were on the same conference calls, and we became friends over that time. Nancy was doing the Law of Attraction as we studied it, to heal her body, and then the two of us had Skype calls every two weeks leading up to the court case. I was determined to help her be free and not face jail time.

She read, did affirmations, and was coached, and another friend helped her assemble all her paperwork for court in chronological order. Lawyers told her to plead guilty. They said that she can't fight the government. Nancy and I discussed the fact that although she was guilty of leaving the country, she did it for the reasons of caring for herself and her kids. She was suffering from guilt, and I wanted to help her. She had suffered enough, with the accident, no money, and two boys to care for on her own.

I had read a fantastic story in Neville Goddard's book *The Law and the Promise* of a woman who had to go to court and the judge in the court room that day had a reputation of being harsh and stern and the lawyers had told her she had no chance of success. This woman had turned to her imagination, and while the jury was out, she ignored all that and repeated silently to herself, 'The verdict is not guilty' over and over and over. I recounted this story to Nancy, and she took hold of it and applied it to herself. Hearing in her imagination 'the verdict is not guilty,' she said it to the lead up of the court case.

She did what she could to keep her mind on freedom on healing her body and on success so that she could continue to heal and take care of her boys. She affirmed, 'It will all be resolved for the good of all concerned.' She also said, 'The verdict is not guilty.' She went to the ocean and baptised herself, talking to the universe for a successful outcome. She Skyped me that day from the car. It was a powerful conversation. She was brave, about to face court that very next day.

The court asked that first day if she had any prior offenses. Everyone looked around at each other; no one had bothered to check that. So court was rescheduled for the following day, and it bought Nancy a bit more time for organising her paperwork.

Next day, they came to the conclusion that she couldn't do community service since she couldn't walk. Nancy kept quiet and sent love to everyone in the court room, the judge, the lawyers, and all else present. They then decided on a pigeon bracelet to be worn on her good ankle for three months, which meant a curfew of 11 p.m. every day. She continued to send love and said to herself, 'I made a mistake, so don't make them wrong. They are just doing their jobs.' She noticed that they didn't look at her. They were all rushing around not connected to what they were doing, and she asked, 'Had anyone read the paperwork?' It seemed they had breezed over it not taking much of it in.

Someone piped up and said, 'A year's probation? She should go to jail for three months.' Nancy continued saying, 'The verdict is not guilty,' in her head over and over.

So the final result was a pigeon's curfew bracelet for six weeks, probation for six months (from August 2014 to February 2015) (meaning she couldn't leave the country), otherwise jail.

She also has to pay back the money.

No jail for Nancy; sentence was light and bearable.

Now, Nancy and I are working on stage two, the money part. To be continued.

Nancy Joyce Hunter
Life coach & Intuitive
Wildlyjoyfullife.com

My wish is that these stories inspire you to try for yourself to create your dreams, step by step, one small or big dream at a time. Life responds to us. It's like a giant photocopy of our thoughts and feelings and what we are focused on.

The Law of Attraction picks up a signal, a vibrational signal, from each of us and with great precision proceeds to bring everything that is a match to that signal to us. Understanding this is the greatest lesson I have ever learnt, and watching the frequency of my own signal has been a never-ending adventure.

Esther Hicks once said that publishers wanted to edit the word 'vibration' from her books. I too believe that it is the most important word. I will not allow anyone to edit it out, which is why I have chosen self-publishing to retain what a creative person wants the most – to have their work left alone, untouched by those who didn't create it.

When the title of this book came to me, I had no idea Sydney had been referred to as Emerald City. I later found this:

> The origins of "Emerald City" goes back to 1910. Frank Baum wrote the book "Emerald City of OZ". Later on in 1939 the classic movie we all know and love was produced by Metro-Goldwyn-Meyer (MGM).
>
> In the late 80's Australian author David Williamson wrote a play about Sydney called "Emerald City."
>
> As visitors and locals alike approach the exquisite harbour, Opera House and Botanical Gardens they are greeted with the scent of fragrant flowers and deep emerald green lawns.
>
> In 2006 Sydney celebrated the diamond anniversary of the Sydney Harbour Bridge and it was referred to as "a diamond night in Emerald City." Sydney is a glittering jewel in the crown of Australia.
>
> I love you Sydney
> You are my home, my Emerald City

What I would like to add to this is that although some come to Sydney and end up with broken dreams, there are those that do fulfil theirs. Some of those individuals understand 'vibration' and the Law of Attraction and live the fulfilled lives, for one simple reason:

They understand that all along they had inside them.

My greatest heartfelt love

Agnes Vivarelli
Agnesvivarelli.com
Apersonofinterest.com.au
Apersonofinterest2014@gmail.com

Printed in Australia
AUOC02n0757060815
269415AU00001B/1/P